SCALES OF JUSTICE

NUNSPARDON MANOR—elegant home of
the Lacklanders who wish to hide what old Sir
Harold had written in his memoirs...

UPLANDS—a decaying manse where a retired
commander nurses his brandy, and his deeply
wounded pride...

JACOB'S COTTAGE—where old Octavius
Danberry-Phinn surrounds himself with his
cats and his bitterness...

HAMMER FARM—the showcase where Col.
Cartarette exhibits his second wife, a social-
climbing young beauty with a history all her
own...

Old houses, all with old secrets—which would
have remained buried, if *murder* had not suddenly occurred in the valley...

"A handsome bit of craftsmanship—a classical
detective story, with lots of suspects."
—The London *Times*

SCALES OF JUSTICE

Ngaio Marsh

A BERKLEY MEDALLION BOOK
published by
BERKLEY PUBLISHING CORPORATION

For Stella

Little, Brown and Company
34 Beacon Street
Boston, Massachusetts 02106

SBN 425-03551-4

BERKLEY MEDALLION BOOKS are published by
Berkley Publishing Corporation
200 Madison Avenue
New York, N. Y. 10016

BERKLEY MEDALLION BOOK ® TM 757,375

Printed in the United States of America

Berkley Medallion Edition, OCTOBER, 1977

SECOND PRINTING

SCALES OF JUSTICE

CHAPTER I

Swevenings

Nurse Kettle pushed her bicycle to the top of Watt's Hill and there paused. Sweating lightly, she looked down on the village of Swevenings. Smoke rose in cosy plumes from one or two chimneys; roofs cuddled into surrounding greenery. The Chyne, a trout stream, meandered through meadow and coppice and slid blamelessly under two bridges. It was a circumspect landscape. Not a faux-pas, architectural or horticultural, marred the seemliness of the prospect.

"Really," Nurse Kettle thought with satisfaction, "it is as pretty as a picture," and she remembered all the pretty pictures Lady Lacklander had made in irresolute water-colour, some from this very spot. She was reminded, too, of those illustrated maps that one finds in the Underground with houses, trees and occupational figures amusingly dotted about them. Seen from above like this, Swevenings resembled such a map. Nurse Kettle looked down at the orderly pattern of field, hedge, stream and land, and fancifully imposed upon it the curling labels and carefully naive figures that are proper to picture-maps.

From Watt's Hill, Watt's Lane ran steeply and obliquely into the valley. Between the lane and the Chyne was contained a hillside divided into three stripes, each garnished with trees, gardens and a house of considerable age. These properties belonged to three of the principal householders of Swevenings: Mr. Danberry-Phinn, Commander Syce and Colonel Cartarette.

Nurse Kettle's map, she reflected, would have a little picture of Mr. Danberry-Phinn at Jacob's Cottage surrounded by his cats, and one of Commander Syce at Uplands, shooting off his bow and arrow. Next door at Hammer Farm (only it wasn't a farm now but had been much converted) it would show Mrs. Cartarette in a garden chair with a cocktail-shaker, and Rose Catarette, her stepdaughter, gracefully weeding. Her attention sharpened. There, in point of fact, deep down in the actual landscape, *was* Colonel Cartarette himself, a Lilliputian figure, moving along his rented stretch of the Chyne, east of Bottom Bridge, and followed at a respectful distance by his spaniel Skip. His creel was slung over his shoulder and his rod was in his hand.

"The evening rise," Nurse Kettle reflected; "he's after the Old 'Un," and she added to her imaginary map the picture of an enormous trout near Bottom Bridge with a curly label above it bearing a legend: "The Old 'Un."

On the far side of the valley on the private golf course at Nunspardon Manor there would be Mr. George Lacklander, doing a solitary round with a glance (thought the gossip-loving Nurse Kettle) across the valley at Mrs. Cartarette. Lacklander's son, Dr. Mark, would be shown with his black bag in his hand and a stork, perhaps, quaintly flying overhead. And to complete, as it were, the gentry, there would be

8

old Lady Lacklander, bog-bottomed on a sketching stool, and her husband, Sir Harold, on a bed of sickness, alas, in his great room, the roof of which, after the manner of pictorial maps, had been removed to display him.

In the map it would be demonstrated how Watt's Lane, wandering to the right and bending back again, neatly divided the gentry from what Nurse Kettle called the "ordinary folk." To the west lay the Danberry-Phinn, the Syce, the Cartarette and above all the Lacklander demesnes. Neatly disposed along the east margin of Watt's Lane were five conscientiously preserved thatched cottages, the village shop and across Monk's Bridge, the church and rectory and the Boy and Donkey.

And that was all. No Pulls-In for Carmen, no Olde Bunne Shoppes (which Nurse Kettle had learned to despise), no spurious half-timbering marred the perfection of Swevenings. Nurse Kettle, bringing her panting friends up to the top of Watt's Hill, would point with her little finger at the valley and observe triumphantly, " 'Where every prospect pleases,' " without completing the quotation, because in Swevenings not even Man was Vile.

With a look of pleasure on her shining and kindly face she mounted her bicycle and began to coast down Watt's Lane. Hedges and trees flew by. The road surface improved and on her left appeared the quickset hedge of Jacob's Cottage. From the far side came the voice of Mr. Octavius Danberry-Phinn.

"Adorable!" Mr. Danberry-Phinn was saying. "Queen of Delight! Fish!" He was answered by the trill of feline voices.

Nurse Kettle turned to the footpath, dexterously

9

backpeddalled, wobbled uncouthly and brought herself to anchor at Mr. Danberry-Phinn's gate.

"Good evening," she said, clinging to the gate and retaining her seat. She looked through the entrance cut in the deep hedge. There was Mr. Danberry-Phinn in his Elizabethan garden giving supper to his cats. In Swevenings, Mr. Phinn (he allowed his nearer acquaintances to neglect the hyphen) was generally considered to be more than a little eccentric, but Nurse Kettle was used to him and didn't find him at all disconcerting. He wore a smoking cap, tasselled, embroidered with beads and falling to pieces. On top of this was perched a pair of ready-made reading glasses, which he now removed and gaily waved at her.

"You appear," he said, "like some exotic deity mounted on an engine quaintly devised by Inigo Jones. Good evening to you, Nurse Kettle. Pray, what has become of your automobile?"

"She's having a spot of beauty treatment and a minor op'." Mr. Phinn flinched at this relentless breeziness, but Nurse Kettle, unaware of his reaction, carried heartily on, "And how's the world treating you? Feeding your kitties, I see."

"The Persons of the House," Mr. Phinn acquiesced, "now, as you observe, sup. Fatima." he cried, squatting on his plump haunches, *Femme fatale*. Miss Paddy-Paws! A morsel more of haddock? Eat up, my heavenly felines." Eight cats of varying kinds responded but slightly to these overtures, being occupied with eight dishes of haddock. The ninth, a mother cat, had completed her meal and was at her toilet. She blinked once at Mr. Phinn and with a tender and gentle expression stretched herself out for the accommodation of her three fat kittens.

"The celestial milk-bar is now open," Mr. Phinn pointed out with a wave of his hand.

Nurse Kettle chuckled obligingly. "No nonsense about *her*, at least," she said. "Pity some human mums I could name haven't got the same idea," she added with an air of professional candour. "Clever pussy!"

"The name," Mr. Phinn corrected tartly, "is Thomasina Twitchett, Thomasina modulating from Thomas and arising out of the usual mistake and Twitchett . . ." He bared his crazy-looking head. *"Hommage a la Divine Potter.* The boy-children are Ptolemy Alexis. The girl-child who suffers from a marked mother-fixation is Edie."

"Edie?" Nurse Kettle repeated doubtfully.

"Edie Puss, of course," Mr. Phinn rejoined and looked fixedly at her.

Nurse Kettle, who knew that one must cry out against puns, ejaculated, "How you *dare! Honestly!"*

Mr. Phinn gave a short cackle of laughter and changed the subject.

"What errand of therapeutic mercy," he asked, "has set you darkling in the saddle? What pain and anguish wring which brow?"

"Well, I've one or two calls," said Nurse Kettle, "but the long and the short of me is that I'm on my way to spend the night at the big house. Relieving with the old gentleman, you know."

She looked across the valley to Nunspardon Manor.

"Ah, yes," said Mr. Phinn softly. "Dear me! May one enquire . . . ? Is Sir Harold . . . ?"

"He's seventy-five," said Nurse Kettle briskly, "and he's very tired. Still, you never know with cardiacs. He may perk up again."

"Indeed?"

"Oh, yes. We've got a day-nurse for him but there's no night-nurse to be had anywhere so I'm stop-gapping. To help Dr. Mark out, really."

"Dr. Mark Lacklander is attending his grand-father?"

"Yes. He had a second opinion but more for his own satisfaction than anything else. But there! Talking out of school! I'm ashamed of you, Kettle."

"I'm very discreet," said Mr. Phinn.

"So'm I, really. Well, I suppose I had better go on me way rejoicing."

Nurse Kettle did a tentative back-pedal and started to wriggle her foot out of the interstices in Mr. Phinn's garden gate. He disengaged a sated kitten from its mother and rubbed it against his ill-shaven cheek.

"Is he conscious?" he asked.

"Off and on. Bit confused. There now! Gossiping again! Talking of gossip," said Nurse Kettle with a twinkle, "I see the Colonel's out for the evening rise."

An extraordinary change at once took place in Mr. Phinn. His face became suffused with purple, his eyes glittered and he bared his teeth in a canine grin.

"A hideous curse upon his sport," he said. "Where is he?"

"Just below the bridge."

"Let him venture a handspan above it and I'll report him to the authorities. What fly has he mounted? Has he caught anything?"

"I couldn't see," said Nurse Kettle, already regretting her part in the conversation, "from the top of Watt's Hill."

Mr. Phinn replaced the kitten.

"It is a dreadful thing to say about a fellow-creature," he said, "a shocking thing. But I do say ad-

12

visedly and deliberately that I suspect Colonel Cartarette of having recourse to improper practices."

It was Nurse Kettle's turn to blush.

"I am sure I don't know to what you refer," she said.

"Bread! Worms!" said Mr. Phinn, spreading his arms. "Anything! Tickling, even! I'd put it as low as that."

"I'm sure you're mistaken."

"It is not my habit, Miss Kettle, to mistake the wanton extravagances of infatuated humankind. Look, if you will, at Cartarette's associates. Look, if your stomach is strong enough to sustain the experience, at Commander Syce."

"Good gracious me, what has the poor Commander done!"

"That man," Mr. Phinn said, turning pale and pointing with one hand to the mother-cat and with the other in the direction of the valley, "that intemperate filibuster, who divides his leisure between alcohol and the idiotic pursuit of archery, that wardroom cupid, my God, murdered the mother of Thomasina Twitchett."

"Not deliberately, I'm sure."

"How can you be sure?"

Mr. Phinn leant over his garden gate and grasped the handlebars of Nurse Kettle's bicycle. The tassel of his smoking cap fell over his face and he blew it impatiently aside. His voice began to trace the pattern of a much-repeated, highly relished narrative.

"In the cool of the evening Madame Thoms, for such was her name, was wont to promenade in the bottom meadow. Being great with kit, she presented a considerable target. Syce, flushed no doubt with wine, and flattering himself he cut the devil of a figure, is to be pictured upon his archery lawn. The instrument of destruction, a bow with the drawing-power, I am told, of sixty pounds, in in his grip and the lust of blood in his heart. He shot an arrow in the air," Mr. Phinn concluded, "and if you tell me that it fell to earth he knew not where, I shall flatly refuse to believe you. His target, his deliberate mark, I am persuaded, was my exquisite cat. Thomasina, my fur of furs, I am speaking of your mama."

The mother-cat blinked at Mr. Phinn and so did Nurse Kettle.

"I must *say*," she thought, "he really *is* a little off," and since she had a kind heart, she was filled with a vague pity for him.

"Living alone," she thought, "with only those cats. It's not to be wondered at, really."

She gave him her brightest professional smile and one of her standard valedictions.

"Ah, well," said Nurse Kettle, letting go her anchorage on the gate, "be good, and if you can't be good, be careful."

"Care," Mr. Danberry-Phinn countered with a look of real intemperance in his eye, "killed the cat. I am not likely to forget it. Good evening to you, Nurse Kettle."

2

Mr. Phinn was a widower, but Commander Syce was a bachelor. He lived next to Mr. Phinn in a Georgian house called Uplands, small and yet too big for Commander Syce, who had inherited it from an uncle. He was looked after by an ex-naval rating and his wife. The greater part of the grounds had been allowed to run to seed, but the kitchen-garden was kept up by the married couple and the archery lawn by Commander Syce himself. It overlooked the valley of the Chyne and was, apparently, his only interest. At one end in fine weather, stood a target on an easel, and at the other on summer evenings, from as far away as Nunspardon, Commander Syce could be observed, in the classic pose, shooting a round from his sixty-pound bow. He was reputed to be a fine marksman, and it was noticed that however much his gait might waver, his stance, once he had opened his chest and stretched his bow, was that of a rock. He lived a solitary and aimless life. People would have inclined to be sorry for him if he had made any sign that he would welcome their sympathy. He did not do so and indeed at the smallest attempt at friendliness would sheer off, go about and make away as fast as possible. Although never seen in the bar, Commander Syce was a heroic supporter of the pub. Indeed, as Nurse Kettle pedalled up his overgrown drive, she encountered the lad from the Boy and Donkey pedalling down it with his bottle-carrier empty before him.

"There's the Boy," thought Nurse Kettle, rather pleased with herself for putting it that way, "and I'm very much afraid he's just paid a visit to the Donkey."

She, herself, had a bottle for Commander Syce, but it came from the chemist at Chyning. As she approached the house, she heard the sound of steps on the gravel and saw him limping away round the far end, his bow in his hand and his quiver girt about his waist. Nurse Kettle pedalled after him.

"Hi!" she called out brightly. "Good evening, Commander!"

Her bicycle wobbled and she dismounted.

Syce turned, hesitated for a moment and then came towards her.

He was a fairish, sunburned man who had run to seed. He still reeked of the navy and, as Nurse Kettle noticed when he drew nearer, of whisky. His eyes, blue and bewildered, stared into hers.

"Sorry," he said rapidly. "Good evening. I beg your pardon."

"Dr. Mark," she said, "asked me to drop in while I was passing and leave your prescription for you. There we are. The mixture as before."

He took it from her with a darting movement of his hand. "Most awfully kind," he said. "Frightfully sorry. Nothing urgent."

"No bother at all," Nurse Kettle rejoined, noticing the tremor of his hand. "I see you're going to have a shoot."

"Oh, yes. Yes," he said loudly, and backed away from her. "Well thank you, thank you, thank you."

"I'm calling in at Hammer. Perhaps you won't mind my trespassing. There's a footpath down to the right-of-way, isn't there?"

"Of course. Please do. Allow me."

He thrust his medicine into a pocket of his coat, took hold of her bicycle and laid his bow along the saddle and handlebars.

"Now *I'm* being the nuisance," said Nurse Kettle cheerfully. "Shall I carry your bow?"

He shied away from her and began to wheel the bicycle round the end of the house. She followed him, carrying the bow and talking in the comfortable voice she used for nervous patients. They came out on the archery lawn and upon a surprising and lovely view over the little valley of the Chyne. The trout stream shone like pewter in the evening light, meadows lay as rich as velvet on either side, the trees looked like pincushions, and a sort of heraldic glow turned the whole landscape into the semblance of an illuminated illustration to some forgotten romance. There was Major Cartarette winding in his line below Bottom Bridge and there up the hill on the Nunspardon golf course were old Lady Lacklander and her elderly son George, taking a postprandial stroll.

"*What* a clear evening," Nurse Kettle exclaimed with pleasure. "And *how* close everything looks. Do tell me, Commander," she went on, noticing that he seemed to flinch at this form of address, "with this bow of yours could you shoot an arrow into Lady Lacklander?"

Syce darted a look at the almost square figure across the little valley. He muttered something about a clout at two hundred and forty yards and limped on. Nurse Kettle, chagrined by his manner, thought, "What you need, my dear, is a bit of gingering up."

He pushed her bicycle down an untidy path through an overgrown shrubbery and she stumped after him.

"I have been told," she said, "that once upon a time you hit a mark you didn't bargain for, down there."

Syce stopped dead. She saw that beads of sweat had formed on the back of his neck. "Alcoholic," she thought. "Flabby. Shame. He must have been a fine man when he looked after himself!"

"Great grief!" Syce cried out, thumping his fist on the seat of her bicycle. "You mean the bloody cat!"

"Well!"

"Great grief, it was an accident. I've told the old perisher! An accident! I *like* cats."

17

He swung round and faced her. His eyes were misted and his lips trembled. "I *like* cats," he repeated.

"We all make mistakes," said Nurse Kettle, comfortably.

He held his hand out for the bow and pointed to a little gate at the end of the path.

"There's the gate into Hammer," he said, and added with exquisite awkwardness, "I beg your pardon; I'm very poor company as you see. Thank you for bringing the stuff. Thank you, thank you."

She gave him the bow and took charge of her bicycle. "Dr. Mark Lacklander may be very young," she said bluffly, "but he's as capable a G.P. as I've come across in thirty years' nursing. If I were you, Commander, I'd have a good down-to-earth chinwag with him. Much obliged for the assistance. Good evening to you."

She pushed her bicycle through the gate into the well-tended coppice belonging to Hammer Farm and along a path that ran between herbaceous borders. As she made her way towards the house, she heard behind her at Uplands the twang of a bowstring and the "tock" of an arrow in a target.

"Poor chap," Nurse Kettle muttered, partly in a huff and partly compassionate. "Poor chap! Nothing to keep him out of mischief," and with a sense of vague uneasiness she wheeled her bicycle in the direction of the Cartarettes' rose garden, where she could hear the snip of garden secateurs and a woman's voice quietly singing.

"That'll be either *Mrs.*," thought Nurse Kettle, "or the stepdaughter. Pretty tune."

A man's voice joined in, making a second part.

Come away, come away, death,
And in sad cypress let me be laid.

The words, thought Nurse Kettle, were a trifle morbid, but the general effect was nice. The rose garden was enclosed behind quickset hedges and hidden from her, but the path she had taken led into it, and she must continue if she was to reach the house. Her rubber-shod feet made little sound on the flagstones, and the bicycle discreetly clicked along beside her. She had an odd feeling that she was about to break in on a scene of exquisite intimacy. She approached a green archway, and as she did so, the woman's voice broke off from its song and said, "That's my favourite of all."

"Strange," said a man's voice that fetched Nurse Kettle up with a jolt, "strange, isn't it, in a comedy, to make the love song so sad! Don't you think so, Rose? Rose . . . Darling . . ."

Nurse Kettle tinkled her bicycle bell, passed through the green archway and looked to her right. She discovered Miss Rose Cartarette and Dr. Mark Lacklander gazing into each other's eyes with unmistakable significance.

3

Miss Cartarette had been cutting roses and laying them in the basket held by Dr. Lacklander. Dr. Lacklander blushed to the roots of his hair and said, "Good God! Good heavens! Good evening," and Miss Cartarette said, "Oh, hullo, Nurse. Good evening." She, too, blushed, but more delicately than Dr. Lacklander.

Nurse Kettle said, "Good evening, Miss Rose. Good

evening, Doctor. Hope it's all right my taking the short cut." She glanced with decorum at Dr. Lacklander. "The child with the abscess," she said, in explanation of her own appearance.

"Ah, yes," Dr. Lacklander said. "I've had a look at her. It's your gardener's little girl, Rose."

They both began to talk to Nurse Kettle, who listened with an expression of good humour. She was a romantic woman and took pleasure in the look of excitement on Dr. Lacklander's face and of shyness on Rose's.

"Nurse Kettle," Dr. Lacklander said rapidly, "like a perfect angel, is going to look after my grandfather tonight. I don't know what we should have done without her."

"*And* by that same token," Nurse Kettle added, "I'd better go on me way rejoicing or I shall be late on duty."

They smiled and nodded at her. She squared her shoulders, glanced in a jocular manner at her bicycle and stumped off with it through the rose garden.

"Well," she thought, "if that's not a case, I've never seen young love before. Blow me down flat, but I never guessed! Fancy!"

As much refreshed by this incident as she would have been by a good strong cup of tea, she made her way to the gardener's cottage, her last port of call before going up to Nunspardon.

When her figure, stoutly clad in her District Nurse's uniform, had bobbed its way out of the enclosed garden, Rose Cartarette and Mark Lacklander looked at each other and laughed nervously.

Lacklander said, "She's a fantastically good sort, old Kettle, but at that particular moment I could have done without her. I mustn't stay, I suppose.

"Don't you want to see papa?"

"Yes. But I shouldn't wait. Not that one can do anything much for the grandparent, but they like me to be there."

"I'll tell Daddy as soon as he comes in. He'll go up at once, of course."

"We'd be very grateful. Grandfather sets great store by his coming."

Mark Lacklander looked at Rose over the basket he carried and said unsteadily, "Darling."

"Don't," she said. "Honestly; don't."

"No? Are you warning me off, Rose? Is it all a dead loss?"

She made a small ineloquent gesture, tried to speak and said nothing.

"Well," Lacklander said, "I may as well tell you that I was going to ask if you'd marry me. I love you dearly, and I thought we seemed to sort of suit. Was I wrong about that?"

"No," Rose said.

"Well, I know I wasn't. Obviously, we suit. So for pity's sake what's up? Don't tell me you love me like a brother, because I can't believe it."

"You needn't try to."

"Well, then?"

"I can't think of getting engaged, much less married."

"Ah!" Lacklander ejaculated. "Now, we're coming to it! This is going to be what I suspected. O, for God's sake let me get rid of this bloody basket! Here. Come over to the bench. I'm not going till I've cleared this up."

She followed him and they sat down together on a

garden seat with the basket of roses at their feet. He took her by the wrist and stripped the heavy glove off her hand. "Now, tell me," he demanded, "do you love me?"

"You needn't bellow it at me like that. Yes, I do."

"Rose, darling! I was so panicked you'd say you didn't."

"Please listen, Mark. You're not going to agree with a syllable of this, but please listen."

"All right, I know what it's going to be but . . . all right."

"You can see what it's like here. I mean the domestic set-up. You must have seen for yourself how much difference it makes to Daddy my being on tap."

"You are so funny when you use colloquialisms . . . a little girl shutting her eyes and firing off a pop-gun. All right; your father likes to have you about. So he well might and so he still would if we married. We'd probably live half our time at Nunspardon."

"It's much more than that." Rose hesitated. She had drawn away from him and sat with her hands pressed together between her knees. She wore a long house-dress. Her hair was drawn back into a knot at the base of her neck, but a single fine strand had escaped and shone on her forehead. She used very little make-up and could afford this economy for she was a beautiful girl.

She said, "It's simply that his second marriage hasn't been a success. If I left him now he'd really and truly have nothing to live for. Really."

"Nonsense," Mark said uneasily.

"He's never been able to do without me. Even when I was little. Nanny and I and my governess all following the drum. So many countries and journeys. And then after the war when he was given all those special jobs—Vienna and Rome and Paris. I never went to school, because he hated the idea of separation."

"All wrong, of course. Only half a life."

"No, no, no, that's not true, honestly. It was a wonderfully rich life. I saw and heard and learnt all sorts of splendid things other girls miss."

"All the same . . ."

"No, honestly, it was grand."

"You shouldn't have been allowed to get under your own steam."

"It wasn't a case of being allowed! I was allowed almost anything I wanted. And when I did get under my own steam just see what happened! He was sent with that mission to Singapore and I stayed in Grenoble and took a course at the university. He was delayed and delayed . . . and I found out afterwards that he was wretchedly at a loose end. And then . . . it was while he was there . . . he met Kitty."

Lacklander closed his well-kept doctor's hand over the lower half of his face and behind it made an indeterminate sound.

"Well," Rose said, "it turned out as badly as it possibly could, and it goes on getting worse, and if I'd been there I don't think it would have happened."

"Why not? He'd have been just as likely to meet her. And even if he hadn't, my heavenly and darling Rose, you cannot be allowed to think of yourself as a twister of the tail of fate."

"If I'd been there . . ."

"Now *look* here!" said Lacklander. "Look at it like this. If you removed yourself to Nunspardon as my wife, he and your stepmother might get together in a quick come-back."

"O, no," Rose said. "No, Mark. There's not a chance of that."

"How do you know? Listen. We're in love. I love you so desperately much it's almost more than I can endure. I know I shall never meet anybody else who could make me so happy and, incredible though it may seem, I don't believe you will either. I won't be put off, Rose. You shall marry me and if your father's life here is too unsatisfactory, well, we'll find some way of improving it. Perhaps if they part company he could come to us."

"Never! Don't you see! He couldn't bear it. He'd feel sort of extraneous."

"I'm going to talk to him. I shall tell him I want to marry you."

"No, Mark, darling! No . . . please . . ."

His hand closed momentarily over hers. Then he was on his feet and had taken up the basket of roses. "Good evening, Mrs. Cartarette," he said. "We're robbing your garden for my grandmother. You're very much ahead of us at Hammer with your roses."

Kitty Cartarette had turned in by the green archway and was looking thoughtfully at them.

4

The second Mrs. Cartarette did not match her Edwardian name. She did not look like a Kitty. She was so fair that without her make-up she would have seemed bleached. Her figure was well disciplined and her face had been skilfully drawn up into a beautifully cared-for mask. Her greatest asset was her acquired inscrutability. This, of itself, made a *femme fatale* of Kitty Cartarette. She had, as it were, been manipulated

24

into a menace. She was dressed with some elaboration and, presumably because she was in the garden, she wore gloves.

"How nice to see you, Mark," she said. "I thought I heard your voices. Is this a professional call?"

Mark said, "Partly so at least. I ran down with a message for Colonel Cartarette, and I had a look at your gardener's small girl."

"How too kind," she said, glancing from Mark to her stepdaughter. She moved up to him and with her gloved hand took a dark rose from the basket and held it against her mouth.

"What a smell!" she said. "Almost improper, it's so strong. Maurice is not in, he won't be long. Shall we go up?"

She led the way to the house. Exotic wafts of something that was not roses drifted in her wake. She kept her torso rigid as she walked and slightly swayed her hips. "Very expensive," Mark Lacklander thought, "but not entirely exclusive. Why on earth did he marry her?"

Mrs. Cartarette's pin heels tapped along the flagstone path to a group of garden furniture heaped with cushions. A tray with a decanter and brandy glasses was set out on a white iron table. She let herself down on a swinging seat, put up her feet, and arranged herself for Mark to look at.

"Poorest Rose," she said, glancing at her stepdaughter, "you're wearing such suitable gloves. Do cope with your scratchy namesakes for Mark. A box perhaps."

"Please don't bother," Mark said. "I'll take them as they are."

"We can't allow that," Mrs. Cartarette murmured.

"You doctors mustn't scratch your lovely hands, you know."

Rose took the basket from him. He watched her go into the house and turned abruptly at the sound of Mrs. Cartarette's voice.

"Let's have a little drink, shall we?" she said. "That's Maurice's pet brandy and meant to be too wonderful. Give me an infinitesimal drop and yourself a nice big one. I really prefer *creme de menthe*, but Maurice and Rose think it a common taste, so I have to restrain my carnal appetite."

Mark gave her the brandy. "I won't, if you don't mind," he said. "I'm by way of being on duty."

"Really? Who are you going to hover over, apart from the gardener's child?"

"My grandfather," Mark said.

"How awful of me not to realize," she rejoined with the utmost composure. "How is Sir Harold?"

"Not so well this evening. I'm afraid. In fact I must get back. If I go by the river path, perhaps I'll meet the Colonel."

"Almost sure to I should think," she agreed indifferently, "unless he's poaching for that fable fish on Mr. Phinn's preserves, which, of course, he's much to county to think of doing, whatever the old boy may say to the contrary."

Mark said formally, "I'll go that way, then, and hope to see him."

She waved her rose at him in dismissal and held out her left hand in a gesture that he found distressingly second-rate. He took it with his own left and shook it crisply.

"Will you give your father a message for me?" she said "I know how worried he must be about your grandfather. Do tell him I wish so much one could help."

The hand inside the glove gave his a sharp little squeeze and was withdrawn. "Don't forget," she said.

Rose came back with the flowers in a box. Mark thought, "I can't leave her like this, half-way through a proposal, damn it." He said coolly, "Come and meet your father. You don't take enough exercise."

"I live in a state of almost perpetual motion," she rejoined, "and I'm not suitably shod or dressed for the river path."

Mrs. Cartarette gave a little laugh. "Poor Mark!" she murmured. "But in any case, Rose, here *comes* your father."

Colonel Cartarette had emerged from a spinney half-way down the hill and was climbing up through the rough grass below the lawn. He was followed by his spaniel Skip, an old, obedient dog. The evening light had faded to a bleached greyness. Stivered grass, trees, lawns, flowers and the mildly curving thread of the shadowed trout stream joined in an announcement of oncoming night. Through this setting Colonel Cartarette moved as if he were an expression both of its substance and its spirit. It was as if from the remote past, through a quiet progression of dusks, his figure had come up from the valley of the Chyne.

When he saw the group by the lawn he lifted his hand in greeting. Mark went down to meet him. Rose, aware of her stepmother's heightened curiosity, watched him with profound misgiving.

Colonel Cartarette was a native of Swevenings. His instincts were those of a countryman and he had never quite lost his air of belonging to the soil. His tastes, however, were for the arts and his talents for the conduct of government services in foreign places. This odd assortment of elements had set no particular mark upon their host. It was not until he spoke that something of his personality appeared.

"Good evening, Mark," he called as soon as they were within comfortable earshot of each other. "My dear chap, what do you think! I've damned near bagged the Old 'Un."

"No!" Mark shouted with appropriate enthusiasm.

"I assure you! The old 'Un! below the bridge in his usual lurk, you know. I could see him. . . ."

And as he panted up the hill, the Colonel completed his classic tale of a magnificent strike, a Homeric struggle and a broken cast. Mark, in spite of his own preoccupations, listened with interest. The Old 'Un was famous in Swevenings: a trout of magnitude and cunning, the despair and desire of every rod in the district.

". . . so I lost him," the Colonel ended, opening his eyes very wide and at the same time grinning for sympathy at Mark. "What a thing! By Jove, if I'd got him I really believe old Phinn would have murdered me."

"Are you still at war, sir?"

"Afraid so. The chap's impossible, you know. Good God, he's accused me in so many words of poaching. Mad! How's your grandfather?"

Mark said, "He's failing pretty rapidly, I'm afraid. There's nothing we can do. It's on his account I'm here, sir." And he delivered his message.

"I'll come at once," the Colonel said. "Better drive round. Just give me a minute or two to clean up. Come round with me, won't you?"

But Mark felt suddenly that he could not face another encounter with Rose and said he would go home at once by the river path and would prepare his grandfather for the Colonel's arrival.

He stood for a moment looking back through the dusk towards the house. He saw Rose gather up the full skirt of her house-coat and run across the lawn, and he saw her father set down his creel and rod, take off his hat and wait for her, his bald head gleaming. She joined her hands behind his neck and kissed him. They went on towards the house arm-in-arm. Mrs. Cartarette's hammock had begun to swing to and fro.

Mark turned away and walked quickly down into the valley and across Bottom Bridge.

The Old 'Un, with Colonel Cartarette's cast in his jaw, lurked tranquilly under the bridge.

CHAPTER II

Nunspardon

Sir Harold Lacklander watched Nurse Kettle as she
moved about his room. Mark had given him something that had reduced his nightmare of discomfort
and for the moment he seemed to enjoy the tragic self-
importance that is the prerogative of the very ill. He
preferred Nurse Kettle to the day-nurse. She was, after
all, a native of the neighbouring village of Chyning,
and this gave him the same satisfaction as the
knowledge that the flowers on his table came out of
the Nunspardon conservatories.

He knew now that he was dying. His grandson had
not told him in so many words, but he had read the
fact of death in the boy's face and in the behaviour of
his own wife and son. Seven years ago he had been
furious when Mark wished to become a doctor: a
Lacklander and the only grandson. He had made it as
difficult as he could for Mark. But he was glad now to
have the Lacklander nose bending over him and the
Lacklander hands doing the things doctors seemed to
think necessary. He would have taken a sort of
pleasure in the eminence to which approaching death
had raised him if he had not been tormented by the

most grievous of all ills. He had a sense of guilt upon him.

"Long time," he said. He used as few words as possible because with every one he uttered it was as if he squandered a measure of his dwindling capital. Nurse Kettle placed herself where he could see and hear her easily and said, "Doctor Mark says the Colonel will be here quite soon. He's been fishing."

"Luck?"

"I don't know. He'll tell you."

"Old 'n."

"Ah," said Nurse Kettle comfortably, "they won't catch him in a hurry."

The wraith of a chuckle drifted up from the bed and was followed by an anxious sigh. She looked closely at the face that seemed during that day to have receded from its own bones.

"All right?" she asked.

The lacklustre eyes searched hers. "Papers?" the voice asked.

"I found them just where you said. They're on the table over there."

"Here."

"If it makes you feel more comfortable." She moved into the shadows at the far end of the great room and returned carrying a package, tied and sealed, which she put on his bedside table.

"Memoirs," he whispered.

"Fancy," said Nurse Kettle. "There must be a deal of work in them. I think it's lovely to be an author. And now I'm going to leave you to have a little rest."

She bent down and looked at him. He stared back anxiously. She nodded and smiled and then moved away and took up an illustrated paper. For a time there were no sounds in the great bedroom but the breathing of the patient and the rustle of a turned page.

The door opened. Nurse Kettle stood up and put her hands behind her back as Mark Lacklander came into the room. He was followed by Colonel Cartarette.

"All right, Nurse?" Mark asked quietly.

"Pretty much," she murmured. "Fretting. He'll be glad to see the Colonel."

"I'll just have a word with him first."

He walked down the room to the enormous bed. His grandfather stared anxiously up at him and Mark, taking the restless old hand in his, said at once, "Here's the Colonel, Grandfather. You're quite ready for him, aren't you?"

"Yes. Now."

"Right." Mark kept his fingers on his grandfather's wrist. Colonel Cartarette straightened his shoulders and joined him.

"Hullo, Cartarette," said Sir Harold so loudly and clearly that Nurse Kettle made a little exclamation. "Nice of you to come."

"Hullo, sir," said the Colonel, who was by twenty-five years the younger. "Sorry you're feeling so cheap. Mark says you want to see me."

"Yes." The eyes turned towards the bedside table. "Those things," he said. "Take them, will you? Now."

"They're memoirs," Mark said.

"Do you want me to read them?" Cartarette asked, stooping over the bed.

"If you will." There was a pause. Mark put the package into Colonel Cartarette's hands. The old man's eyes watched in what seemed to be an agony of interest.

33

"I think," Mark said, "that Grandfather hopes you will edit the memoirs, sir."

"I'll . . . Of course," the Colonel said after an infinitesimal pause. "I'll be delighted; if you think you can trust me."

"Trust you. Implicitly. Implicitly. One other thing. Do you mind, Mark?"

"Of course not, Grandfather. Nurse, shall we have a word?"

Nurse Kettle followed Mark out of the room. They stood together on a dark landing at the head of a wide stairway.

"I don't think," Mark said, "that it will be much longer."

"Wonderful, though, how he's perked up for the Colonel."

"He'd set his will on it. I think," Mark said, "that he will now relinquish his life."

Nurse Kettle agreed. "Funny how they can hang on and funny how they will give up."

In the hall below a door opened and light flooded up the stairs. Mark looked over the banister and saw the enormously broad figure of his grandmother. Her hand flashed as it closed on the stair rail. She began heavily to ascend. He could hear her labored breathing.

"Steady does it, Gar," he said.

Lady Lacklander paused and looked up. "Ha!" she said. "It's the doctor, is it?" Mark grinned at the sardonic overtone.

She arrived on the landing. The train of her old velvet dinner dress followed her, and the diamonds which every evening she absent-mindedly stuck about her enormous bosom burned and winked as it rose and fell.

"Good evening, Miss Kettle," she panted. "Good of you to come and help my poor old boy. How is he, Mark? Has Maurice Cartarette arrived? Why are you both closeted together out here?"

"The Colonel's here, Gar. Grandfather wanted to have a word privately with him, so Nurse and I left them together."

"Something about those damned memoirs," said Lady Lacklander vexedly. "I suppose, in that case, I'd better not go in."

"I don't think they'll be long."

There was a large Jacobean chair on the landing. He pulled it forward. She let herself down into it, shuffled her astonishingly small feet out of a pair of old slippers and looked critically at them.

"Your father," she said, "has gone to sleep in the drawing-room muttering that he would like to see Maurice." She shifted her great bulk towards Nurse Kettle. "Now, before you settle to your watch, you kind soul," she said, "you won't mind saving my mammoth legs a journey. Jog down to the drawing-room, rouse my lethargic son, tell him the Colonel's here and make him give you a drink and a sandwich. Um?"

"Yes, of course, Lady Lacklander," said Nurse Kettle and descended briskly. "Wanted to get rid of me," she thought, "but it was tactfully done."

"Nice woman, Kettle," Lady Lacklander grunted. "She knows I wanted to be rid of her. Mark, what is it that's making your grandfather unhappy?"

"Is he unhappy, Gar?"

"Don't hedge. He's worried to death. . . ." She

stopped short. Her jewelled hands twitched in her lap. "He's troubled in his mind," she said, "and for the second occasion in our married life I'm at a loss to know why. Is it something to do with Maurice and the memoirs?"

"Apparently. He wants the Colonel to edit them."

"The first occasion," Lady Lacklander muttered, "was twenty years ago and it made me perfectly miserable. And now, when the time has come for us to part company . . . and it has come, child, hasn't it?"

"Yes, darling, I think so. He's very tired."

"I know. And I'm not. I'm seventy-five and grotesquely fat, but I have a zest for life. There are still," Lady Lacklander said with a change in her rather wheezy voice, "there are still things to be tidied up. George, for example."

"What's my poor papa doing that needs a tidying hand?" Mark asked gently.

"Your poor papa," she said, "is fifty and a widower and a Lacklander. Three ominous circumstances."

"Which can't be altered, even by you."

"They can, however, be . . . Maurice! What is it?"

Colonel Cartarette had opened the door and stood on the threshold with the packages still under his arm.

"Can you come, Mark? Quickly."

Mark went past him into the bedroom. Lady Lacklander had risen and followed with more celerity than he would have thought possible. Colonel Cartarette stopped her in the doorway.

"My dear," he said, "wait a moment."

"Not a second," she said strongly. "Let me in, Maurice."

A bell rang persistently in the hall below. Nurse

Kettle, followed by a tall man in evening clothes, came hurrying up the stairs.

Colonel Cartarette stood on the landing and watched them go in.

Lady Lacklander was already at her husband's bedside. Mark supported him with his right arm and with his left hand kept his thumb on a bell-push that lay on the bed. Sir Harold's mouth was open and he was fetching his breath in a series of half-yawns. There was a movement under the bedclothes that seemed to be made by a continuous flexion and extension of his leg. Lady Lacklander stood massively beside him and took both his hands between hers.

"I'm here, Hal," she said.

Nurse Kettle had appeared with a glass in her hand. "Brandy," she said. "Old-fashioned but good."

Mark held it to his grandfather's open mouth. "Try," he said. "It'll help. Try."

The mouth closed over the rim.

"He's got a little," Mark said. "I'll give an injection."

Nurse Kettle took his place. Mark turned away and found himself face-to-face with his father.

"Can I do anything?" George Lacklander asked.

"Only wait here, if you will, Father."

"Here's George, Hal," Lady Lacklander said. "We're all here with you, my dear."

From behind the mask against Nurse Kettle's shoulder came a stutter, "Vic—Vic . . . Vic," as if the pulse that was soon to run down had become semi-articulate like a clock. They looked at each other in dismay.

"What is it?" Lady Lacklander asked. "What is it, Hal?"

"Somebody called Vic?" Nurse Kettle suggested brightly.

"There is nobody called Vic," said George Lacklander and sounded impatient. "For God's sake, Mark, can't you help him?"

"In a moment," Mark said from the far end of the room.

"Vic . . ."

"The vicar?" Lady Lacklander asked, pressing his hand and bending over him. "Do you want the vicar to come, Hal?"

His eyes stared up into hers. Something like a smile twitched at the corners of the gaping mouth. The head moved slightly.

Mark came back with the syringe and gave the injection. After a moment Nurse Kettle moved away. There was something in her manner that gave definition to the scene. Lady Lacklander and her son and grandson drew closer to the bed. She had taken her husband's hands again.

"What is it, Hal? What is it, my dearest?" she asked. "Is it the vicar?"

With a distinctness that astonished them he whispered, "After all, you never know," and with his gaze still fixed on his wife he then died.

2

On the late afternoon three days after his father's funeral, Sir George Lacklander sat in the study at Nunspardon going through the contents of the files and the desk. He was a handsome man with a look of conventional distinction. He had been dark but was now grizzled in the most becoming way possible with grey wings at his temples and a plume above his forehead. Inevitably, his mouth was firm and the nose above it appropriately hooked. He was, in short, rather like an illustration of an English gentleman in an American magazine. He had arrived at the dangerous age for such men, being now fifty years old and remarkably vigorous.

Sir Harold had left everything in apple-pie order, and his son anticipated little trouble. As he turned over the pages of his father's diaries, it occurred to him that as a family they richly deserved their too-much-publicized nicknames of "Lucky Lacklanders." How lucky, for instance, that the eighth baronet, an immensely wealthy man, had developed a passion for precious stones and invested in them to such an extent that they constituted a vast realizable fortune in themselves. How lucky that their famous racing stables were so phenomenally successful. How uniquely and fantastically lucky had been in that no fewer than three times in the past century a Lacklander had won the most famous of all sweepstakes. It was true, of course, that he himself might be said to have had a piece of ill-fortune when his wife had died in giving birth to Mark, but as he remembered her, and he had to confess he no longer remembered her at all distinctly, she had been a disappointingly dull woman. Nothing like . . . But here he checked himself smartly and swept up his moustache with his thumb and forefinger. He was disconcerted when at this precise moment the butler came in to say that Colonel Cartarette had called and would like to see him. In a vague way the visit suggested a judgment. He took up a firm position on the hearthrug.

"Hullo, Maurice," he said when the Colonel came

in. "Glad to see you." He looked self-consciously into the Colonel's face and with a changed voice said, "Anything wrong?"

"Well, yes," the Colonel said. "A hell of a lot actually. I'm sorry to bother you, George, so soon after your trouble and all that, but the truth is I'm so damned worried that I feel I've got to share my responsibility with you."

"Me!" Sir George ejaculated, apparently with relief and a kind of astonishment. The Colonel took two envelopes from his pocket and laid them on the desk. Sir George saw that they were addressed in his father's writing.

"Read the letter first," the Colonel said, indicating the smaller of the two envelopes. George gave him a wondering look. He screwed in his eyeglass, drew a single sheet of paper from the envelope, and began to read. As he did so, his mouth fell gently open and his expression grew increasingly blank. Once he looked up at the troubled Colonel as if to ask a question but seemed to change his mind and fell again to reading.

At last the paper dropped from his fingers and his monocle from his eye to his waistcoat.

"I don't," he said, "understand a word of it."

"You will," the Colonel said, "when you have looked at this." He drew a thin sheaf of manuscript out of the larger envelope and placed it before George Lacklander. "It will take you ten minutes to read. If you don't mind, I'll wait."

"My dear fellow! Do sit down. What am I thinking of. A cigar! A drink."

"No thank you, George. I'll smoke a cigarette. No, don't move. I've got one."

George gave him a wondering look, replaced his eyeglass and began to read again. As he did so, his face went through as many changes of expression as those depicted in strip-advertisements. He was a rubicund man, but the fresh colour drained out of his face. His mouth lost its firmness and his eyes their assurance. When he raised a sheet of manuscript, it quivered in his grasp.

Once, before he had read to the end, he did speak. "But it's not true," he said. "We've always known what happened. It was well known." He touched his lips with his fingers and read on to the end. When the last page had fallen on the others, Colonel Cartarette gathered them up and put them into their envelope.

"I'm damned sorry, George," he said. "God knows I didn't want to land you with all this."

"I can't see, now, why you've done it. Why bring it to me? Why do anything but throw it at the back of the fire?"

Cartarette said sombrely, "I see you haven't listened to me. I told you. I've thought it over very carefully. He's left the decision with me and I've decided I must publish . . ." he held up the long envelope . . . "this. I must, George. Any other course would be impossible."

"But have you thought what it will do to us? Have you thought? It . . . it's *un*thinkable. You're an old friend, Maurice. My father trusted you with this business because he thought of you as a friend. In a way," George added, struggling with an idea that was a little too big for him, "in a way he's bequeathed you our destiny."

"A most unwelcome legacy if it were so, but of course it's not. You're putting it altogether too high. I

41

know, believe me, George, I know, how painful and distressing this will be to you all, but I think the public will take a more charitable view than you might suppose."

"And since when," George demanded with a greater command of rhetoric than might have been expected of him, "since when have the Lacklanders stood cap-in-hand, waiting upon the charity of the public?"

Colonel Cartarette's response to this was a helpless gesture. "I'm terribly sorry," he said, "but I'm afraid that that sentiment has the advantage of sounding well and meaning nothing."

"Don't be so bloody supercilious."

"All right, George, all right."

"The more I think of this the worse it gets. Look here, Maurice, if for no other reason, in common decency . . ."

"I've tried to take common decency as my criterion."

"It'll kill my mother."

"It will distress her very deeply, I know. I've thought of her, too."

"And Mark? Ruin! A young man! My son! Starting his career."

"There was another young man, an only son, who was starting on his career."

"He's dead!" George cried out. "He can't suffer. He's dead."

"And *his* name? And *his* father?"

"I can't chop logic with you. I'm a simple sort of bloke with, I daresay, very unfashionable standards. I believe in the loyalty of friends and in the old families sticking together."

"At whatever the cost to other friends and other old families? Come off it, George," said the Colonel.

The colour flooded back into George's face until it was empurpled. He said in an unrecognizable voice, "Give me my father's manuscript. Give me that envelope. I demand it."

"I can't, old boy. Good God, do you suppose that if I could chuck it away or burn it with anything like a clear conscience I wouldn't do it? I tell you I hate this job."

He returned the envelope to the breast pocket of his coat. "You're free, of course," he said, "to talk this over with Lady Lacklander and Mark. Your father made no reservations about that. By the way, I've brought a copy of his letter in case you decide to tell them about it. Here it is." The Colonel produced a third envelope, laid it on the desk and moved towards the door. "And George," he said, "I beg you to believe I am sorry. I'm deeply sorry. If I could see any other way, I'd thankfully take it. What?"

George Lacklander had made an inarticulate noise. He now pointed a heavy finger at the Colonel.

"After this," he said, "I needn't tell you that any question of an understanding between your girl and my boy is at an end."

The Colonel was so quiet for so long that both men became aware of the ticking of the clock on the chimney breast.

"I didn't know," he said at last, "that there was any question of an understanding. I think you must be mistaken."

"I assure you that I am not. However, we needn't discuss it. Mark . . . and Rose, I am sure . . . will both see that it is quite out of the question. No doubt you are as ready to ruin her chances as you are to destroy our happiness." For a moment he watched the Colonel's blank face. "She's head over heels in love with him," he added; "you can take my word for it."

"If Mark has told you this . . ."

"Who says Mark told me? . . . I . . . I . . ."

The full, rather florid voice faltered and petered out.

"Indeed," the Colonel said. "Then may I ask where you got your information?"

They stared at each other and, curiously, the look of startled conjecture which had appeared on George Lacklander's face was reflected on the Colonel's. "It couldn't matter less, in any case," the Colonel said. "Your informant, I am sure, is entirely mistaken. There's no point in my staying. Goodbye."

He went out. George, transfixed, saw him walk past the window. A sort of panic came over him. He dragged the telephone across his desk and with an unsteady hand dialled Colonel Cartarette's number. A woman's voice answered.

"Kitty!" he said. "Kitty, is that you?"

3

Colonel Cartarette went home by the right-of-way known as the River Path. It ran through Nunspardon from the top end of Watt's Lane skirting the Lacklander's private golf course. It wound down to Bottom Bridge and up the opposite side to the Cartarette's spinney. From thence it crossed the lower portion of Commander Syce's and Mr. Phinn's demesnes and rejoined Watt's Lane just below the crest of Watt's Hill.

The Colonel was feeling miserable. He was weighed

down by his responsibility and upset by his falling out with George Lacklander, who, pompous old ass though the Colonel thought him, was a lifetime friend. Worst of all, he was wretchedly disturbed by the suggestion that Rose had fallen in love with Mark and by the inference, which he couldn't help drawing, that George Lacklander had collected this information from the Colonel's wife.

As he walked down the hillside, he looked across the little valley into the gardens of Jacob's Cottage, Uplands and Hammer Farm. There was Mr. Phinn dodging about with a cat on his shoulder: "like a blasted old warlock," thought the Colonel, who had fallen out with Mr. Phinn over the trout stream, and there was poor Syce blazing away with his bow and arrow at his padded target. And there, at Hammer, was Kitty. With a characteristic movement of her hips she had emerged from the house in skintight velvet trousers and a flame-coloured top. Her long cigarette-holder was in her hand. She seemed to look across the valley at Nunspardon. The Colonel felt a sickening jolt under his diaphragm. "How I could!" he thought (though subconsciously). "How I could!" Rose was at her evening employment cutting off the deadheads in the garden. He sighed and looked up to the crest of the hill, and there plodding homewards, pushing her bicycle up Watt's Lane, her uniform and hat appearing in gaps and vanishing behind hedges, was Nurse Kettle. "In Swevenings," thought the Colonel, "she crops up like a recurring decimal."

He came to the foot of the hill and to the Bottom Bridge. The bridge divided his fishing from Mr. Danberry-Phinn's: he had the lower reaches and Mr.

Phinn the upper. It was about the waters exactly under Bottom Bridge that they had fallen out. The Colonel crossed from Mr. Phinn's side to his own, folded his arms on the stone parapet and gazed into the sliding green world beneath. At first he stared absently, but after a moment his attention sharpened. In the left bank of the Chyne near a broken-down boatshed where an old punt was moored, there was a hole. In its depths eddied and lurked a shadow among shadows: the Old 'Un. "Perhaps," the Colonel thought, "perhaps it would ease my mind a bit if I came down before dinner. He may stay on my side." He withdrew his gaze from the Old 'Un to find, when he looked up at Jacob's Cottage, that Mr. Phinn, motionless, with his cat still on his shoulder, was looking at him through a pair of field-glasses.

"Ah hell!" muttered the Colonel. He crossed the bridge and passed out of sight of Jacob's Cottage and continued on his way home.

The path crossed a narrow meadow and climbed the lower reach of Watt's Hill. His own coppice and Commander Syce's spinney concealed from the Colonel the upper portions of the three demesnes. Someone was coming down the path at a heavy jog-trot. He actually heard the wheezing and puffing of this person and recognized the form of locomotion practised by Mr. Phinn before the latter appeared wearing an old Norfolk jacket and tweed hat which, in addition to being stuck with trout-fishing flies, had Mr. Phinn's reading spectacles thrust through the band like an Irishman's pipe. He was carrying his elaborate collection of fishing impedimenta. He had the air of having got himself together in a hurry and was attended by

Mrs. Thomasina Twitchett, who, after the manner of her kind, suggested that their association was purely coincidental.

The path was narrow. It was essential that someone should give way and the Colonel, sick of rows with his neighbours, stood on one side. Mr. Phinn jogged glassily down upon him. The cat suddenly cantered ahead.

"Hullo, old girl," said the Colonel. He stooped down and snapped a finger and thumb at her. She stared briefly and passed him with a preoccupied air, twitching the tip of her tail.

The Colonel straightened up and found himself face-to-face with Mr. Phinn.

"Good evening," said the Colonel.

"Sir," said Mr. Phinn. He touched his dreadful hat with one finger, blew out his cheeks and advanced. "Thomasina," he added, "hold your body more seemly."

For Thomasina, waywardly taken with the Colonel, had returned and rolled on her back at his feet.

"Nice cat," said the Colonel and added, "Good fishing to you. The Old 'Un lies below the bridge on my side, by the way?"

"Indeed?"

"As no doubt you guessed," the Colonel added against his better judgment, "when you watched me through your field-glasses."

If Mr. Phinn had contemplated a conciliatory position, he at once abandoned it. He made a belligerent gesture with his net. "The landscape, so far as I am aware," he said, "is not under some optical interdict. It may be viewed, I believe. To the best of my knowledge, there are no squatter's rights over the distant prospect of the Chyne."

"None whatever. You can stare," said the Colonel, "at the Chyne, or me, or anything else you fancy till you are black in the face, for all I care. But if you realized . . . If you . . ." He scratched his head, a gesture that with the Colonel denoted profound emotional disturbance. "My dear Phinn . . ." he began again, "if you only knew . . . God bless my soul, what *does* it matter! Good evening to you."

He encircled Mr. Phinn and hurried up the path. "And for that grotesque," he thought resentfully, "for that impossible, that almost certifiable buffoon I have saddled myself with a responsibility that well make me wretchedly uncomfortable for the rest of my life."

He mended his pace and followed the path into the Hammer coppice. Whether summoned by maternal obligations or because she had taken an inscrutable cat's fancy to the Colonel, Thomasina Twitchett accompanied him, trilling occasionally and looking about for an evening bird. They came within view of the lawn, and there was Commander Syce, bow in hand, quiver at thigh and slightly unsteady on his feet, hunting about in the underbrush.

"Hullo, Cartarette," he said. "Lost a damned arrow. What a thing! Missed the damned target and away she went."

"Missed it by a dangerously wide margin, didn't you?" the Colonel rejoined rather testily. After all, people did use the path, he reflected, and he began to help in the search. Thomasina Twitchett, amused by the rustle of leaves, pretended to join in the hunt.

48

"I know," Commander Syce agreed; "rotten bad show, but I saw old Phinn and it put me off. Did you hear what happened about me and his cat? Damnedest thing you ever knew! Purest accident, but the old whatnot wouldn't have it. Great grief, I told him, I *like* cats."

He thrust his hand into a heap of dead leaves. Thomasina Twitchett leapt merrily upon it and fleshed her claws in his wrist. "Perishing little bastard," said Commander Syce. He freed himself and aimed a spank at her which she easily avoided and being tired of their company, made for her home and kittens. The Colonel excused himself and turned up through the spinney into the open field below his own lawn.

His wife was in her hammock dangling a tightly encased black-velvet leg, a flame-coloured sleeve and a pair of enormous ear-rings. The cocktail tray was already on her iron table.

"How late you are," she said, idly. "Dinner in half an hour. What have you been up to at Nunspardon?"

"I had to see George."

"What about?"

"Some business his father asked me to do."

"How illuminating."

"It was very private, my dear."

"How *is* George?"

The Colonel remembered George's empurpled face and said, "Still rather upset."

"We must ask him to dinner. I'm learning to play golf with him tomorrow, by the way. He's giving me some clubs. Nice, isn't it?"

"When did you arrange that?"

"Just now. About twenty minutes ago," she said, watching him.

"Kitty, I'd rather you didn't."

"You don't by any chance suspect me of playing you false with George, do you?"

"Well," said the Colonel after a long pause, "are you?"

"No."

"I still think it might be better not to play golf with him tomorrow."

"Why on earth?"

"Kitty. what have you said to George about Mark and Rose?"

"Nothing you couldn't have seen for yourself, darling. Rose is obviously head over heels in love with Mark."

"I don't believe you."

"My good Maurice, you don't suppose the girl is going to spend the rest of her existence doting on Daddy, do you?"

"I wouldn't have it for the world. Not for the world."

"Well, then."

"But I . . . I didn't know . . . I still don't believe . . ."

"He turned up here five minutes ago looking all churned-up, and they're closeted together in the drawing-room. Go and see. I'll excuse your changing, if you like."

"Thank you, my dear," the Colonel said miserably and went indoors.

If he hadn't been so rattled and worried he would no doubt have given some sort of warning of his approach. As it was, he crossed the heavy carpet of the hall, opened the drawing-room door and discovered his daughter locked in Mark Lacklander's arms, from which embrace she was making but ineffectual attempts to escape.

CHAPTER III

The Valley of the Chyne

Rose and Mark behaved in the classic manner of surprised lovers. They released each other. Rose turned white and Mark red, and neither of them uttered a word.

The Colonel said, "I'm sorry, my dear. Forgive me," and made his daughter a little bow.

Rose, with a sort of agitated spontaneity, ran to him, linked her hands behind his head and cried, "It had to happen sometime, darling, didn't it?"

Mark said, "Sir, I want her to marry me."

"But I won't," Rose said, "I won't unless you can be happy about it. I've told him."

The Colonel, with great gentleness, freed himself and then put an arm round his daughter.

"Where have you come from, Mark?" he asked.

"From Chyning. It's my day at the hospital."

"Yes, I see." The Colonel looked from his daughter to her lover and thought how ardent and vulnerable they seemed. "Sit down, both of you," he said. "I've got to think what I'm going to say to you. Sit down."

They obeyed him with an air of bewilderment.

"When you go back to Nunspardon, Mark," he said, "you will find your father very much upset. That is because of a talk I've just had with him. I'm at liberty to repeat the substance of that talk to you, but I feel some hesitation in doing so. I think he should be allowed to break it to you himself."

"*Break* it to me?"

"It is not good news. You will find him entirely opposed to any thought of your marriage with Rose."

"I can't believe it," Mark said.

"You will, however. You may even find that you yourself (forgive me, Rose, my love, but it may be so) feel quite differently about . . ." the Colonel smiled faintly . . . "about contracting an alliance with a Cartarette."

"But, my poorest Daddy," Rose ejaculated, clinging to a note of irony, "what have you been up to?"

"The very devil and all, I'm afraid, my poppet," her father rejoined.

"Well, whatever it may be," Mark said and stood up, "I can assure you that blue murder wouldn't make me change my mind about Rose."

"O," the Colonel rejoined mildly, "this is not blue murder."

"Good." Mark turned to Rose. "Don't be fussed, darling," he said. "I'll go home and sort it out."

"By all means, go home," the Colonel agreed, "and try."

He took Mark by the arm and led him to the door.

"You won't feel very friendly towards me tomorrow, Mark," he said. "Will you try to believe that the action I've been compelled to take is one that I detest taking?"

"Compelled?" Mark repeated. "Yes, well . . . yes, of course." He stuck out the Lacklander jaw and knitted the Lacklander brows. "Look here, sir," he said, "if my father welcomes our engagement . . . and I can't conceive of his doing anything else . . . will you have any objection? I'd better tell you now that no objection on either side will make the smallest difference."

"In that case," the Colonel said, "our question is academic. And now I'll leave you to have a word with Rose before you go home." He held out his hand. "Goodbye, Mark."

When the Colonel had gone, Mark turned to Rose and took her hands in his. "But how ridiculous," he said. "How in the world could these old boys cook up anything that would upset *us?*"

"I don't know. I don't know how they could, but it's serious. He's terribly worried, poor darling."

"Well," Mark said, "it's no good attempting a diagnosis before we've heard the history. I'll go home, see what's happened and ring you up in about fifteen minutes. The all-important, utterly bewildering and Heaven-sent joy is that you love me, Rose. Nothing," Mark continued with an air of coining a brand-new phrase, "nothing can alter that. Au revoir, darling."

He kissed Rose in a business-like manner and was gone.

She sat still for a time hugging to herself the knowledge of their feeling for each other. What had happened to all her scruples about leaving her father? She didn't even feel properly upset by her father's extraordinary behaviour, and when she realized this circumstance, she realized the extent of her exthrallment. She stood in the French window of the drawing-room and looked across the valley to Nunspardon. It was impossible to be anxious . . . her whole being ached with happiness. It was now and for the first time that Rose understood the completeness of love.

Time went by without her taking thought of it. The gong sounded for dinner and at the same moment the telephone rang. She flew to it.

"Rose," Mark said. "Say at once that you love me. At once."

"I love you."

"And on your most sacred word of honour that you'll marry me. Say it, Rose. Promise it. Solemnly promise."

"I solemnly promise."

"Good," said Mark. "I'll come back at nine."

"Do you know what's wrong?"

"Yes. It's damn' ticklish. Bless you, darling. Till nine."

"Till nine," Rose said and in a state of enthrallment went in to dinner.

2

By eight o'clock the evening depression had begun to settle over Commander Syce. At about five o'clock, when the sun was over the yard-arm, he had a brandy and soda. This raised his spirits. With its successors, up to the third or fourth, they rose still further. During this period he saw himself taking a job and making a howling success of it. From that emotional eminence he fell away with each succeeding dram, and it was during his decline that he usually took to archery. It had been in such a state of almost suiciddal depression that he had suddenly shot an arrow over his coppice into Mr. Danberry-Phinn's bottom meadow and slain the mother of Thomasina Twitchett.

To-night the onset of depression was more than usually severe. Perhaps his encounter with the Colonel, whom he liked, gave point to his own loneliness. Moreover, his married couple were on their annual holiday and he had not been bothered to do anything about an evening meal. He found his arrow and limped back to the archery lawn. He no longer wanted to shoot. His gammy leg ached, but he thought he'd take a turn up the drive.

Whe he arrived at the top, it was to discover Nurse Kettle seated by the roadside in gloomy contemplation of her bicycle, which stood upside down on its saddle and handlebars.

"Hullo, Commander," said Nurse Kettle, "I've got a puncture."

"Evening. Really? Bore for you," Syce shot out at her.

"I can't make up me great mind to push her the three miles to Chyning, so I'm going to have a shot at running repairs. Pumping's no good," said Nurse Kettle.

She had opened a tool kit and was looking dubiously at its contents. Syce hung off and on and watched her make a pass with a lever at her tyre.

"Not like that," he shouted when he could no longer endure it. "Great grief, you'll get nowhere that fashion."

"I believe you."

"And in any case you'll want a bucket of water to find the puncture." She looked helplessly at him. "Here!" he mumbled. "Give it here."

He righted the bicycle and with a further, completely inaudible remark began to wheel it down his drive. Nurse Kettle gathered up her tool kit and followed. A look strangely compounded of compassion and amusement had settled on her face.

Commander Syce wheeled the bicycle into a gardener's shed and without the slightest attempt at any further conversation set about the removal of the tyre. Nurse Kettle hitched herself up on a bench and watched him. Presently she began to talk.

"I *am* obliged to you. I've had a bit of a day. Epidemic in the village, odd cases all over the place, and then this happens. There! Aren't you neat-fingered. I looked in at Nunspardon this evening," she continued. "Lady Lacklander's got a 'toe,' and Dr. Mark arranged for me to do the fomentations."

Commander Syce made an inarticulate noise.

"If you ask *me*, the new baronet's feeling his responsibilities. Came in just as I was leaving. Very bad colour and jumpy," Nurse Kettle gossiped cosily. She swung her short legs and interrupted herself from time to time to admire Syce's handiwork. "Pity!" she thought. "Shaky hands. Alcoholic skin. Nice chap, too. Pity!"

He repaired the puncture and replaced the tube and tyre. When he had finished and made as if to stand up, he gave a sharp cry of pain, clapped his hand to the small of his back and sank down again on his knees.

"Hul—lo!" Nurse Kettle ejaculated. "What's all this? 'Bago?"

Commander Syce swore under his breath. Between clenched teeth he implored her to go away. "Most frightfully sorry," he groaned. "Ask you to excuse me. Ach!"

It was now that Nurse Kettle showed the quality that caused people to prefer her to grander and more up-to-date nurses. She exuded dependability, resourcefulness and authority. Even the common and

58

pitilessly breezy flavour of her remarks was comfortable. To Commander Syce's conjurations to leave him alone, followed in the extremity of his pain by furious oaths, she paid no attention. She went down on all fours beside him, enticed and aided him towards the bench, encouraged him to use it and her own person as aids to rising, and finally had him, though almost bent double, on his feet. She helped him into his house and lowered him down on a sofa in a dismal drawing-room.

"Down-a-bumps," she said. Sweating and gasping, he reclined and glared at her. "Now, what are we going to do about *you,* I wonder? Did I or did I not see a rug in the hall? Wait a bit."

She went out and came back with a rug. She called him "dear" and, taking his pain seriously, covered him up, went out again and returned with a glass of water. "Making myself at home, I suppose you're thinking. Here's a couple of aspirins to go on with," said Nurse Kettle.

He took them without looking at her. "Please don't trouble," he groaned. "Thank you. Under my own steam." She gave him a look and went out again.

In her absence, he attempted to get up but was galvanized with a monstrous jab of lumbago and subsided in agony. He began to think she had gone for good and to wonder how he was to support life while the attack lasted, when he heard her moving about in some remote part of the house. In a moment she came in with two hot-water bags.

"At this stage," she said, "heat's the ticket."

"Where did you get those things?"

"Borrowed 'em from the Cartarettes."

"My God!"

She laid them against his back.

"Dr. Mark's coming to look at you," she said.

"My God!"

"He was at the Cartarettes and if you ask me, there's going to be some news from that quarter before any of us are much older. At least," Nurse Kettle added rather vexedly, "I *would* have said so, if it hadn't been for them all looking a bit put out." To his horror she began to take off his shoes.

"With a yo-heave-ho," said Nurse Kettle out of compliment to the navy. "Aspirin doing its stuff?"

"I . . . I think so. I *do beg* . . ."

"I suppose your bedroom's upstairs?"

"I do BEG . . ."

"We'll see what the doctor says, but I'd suggest you doss down in the housekeeper's room to save the stairs. I mean to say," Nurse Kettle added with a hearty laugh, "always provided there's no housekeeper."

She looked into his face so good-humouredly and with such an air of believing him to be glad of her help that he found himself accepting it.

"Like a cup of tea?" she asked.

"No thank you."

"Well, it won't be anything stronger unless the doctor says so."

He reddened, caught her eye and grinned.

"Come," she said, "that's better."

"I'm really ashamed to trouble you so much."

"I might have said the same about my bike, mightn't I? There's the doctor."

She bustled out again and came back with Mark Lacklander.

Mark, who was a good deal paler than his patient, took a crisp line with Syce's expostulations.

"All right," he said. "I daresay I'm entirely extraneous. This isn't a professional visit if you'd rather not."

"Great grief, my dear chap, I don't mean that. Only too grateful but . . . I mean . . . busy man . . . right itself . . ."

"Well, suppose I take a look-see," Mark suggested. "We won't move you."

The examination was brief. "If the lumbago doesn't clear up, we can do something a bit more drastic," Mark said, "but in the meantime Nurse Kettle'll get you to bed . . ."

"Good God!"

". . . and look in again to-morrow morning. So will I. You'll need one or two things; I'll ring up the hospital and get them sent out at once. All right?"

"Thank you. Thank you. You don't," said Syce, to his own surprise, "look terribly fit yourself. Sorry to have dragged you in."

"That's all right. We'll bring your bed in here and put it near the telephone. Ring up if you're in difficulties. By the way, Mrs. Cartarette offered . . ."

"NO!" shouted Commander Syce and turned purple.

". . . to send in meals," Mark added. "But of course you may be up and about again to-morrow. In the meantime I think we can safely leave you to Nurse Kettle. Good-night."

When he had gone, Nurse Kettle said cheerfully, "You'll have to put up with me, it seems, if you don't want lovely ladies all round you. Now we'll get you washed up and settled for the night."

Half an hour later when he was propped up in bed with a cup of hot milk and a plate of bread and butter and the lamp within easy reach, Nurse Kettle looked down at him with her quizzical air.

"Well," she said, "I shall now, as they say, love you and leave you. Be good and if you can't be good, be careful."

"Thank you," gabbled Commander Syce, nervously. "Thank you, thank you, thank you."

She had plodded over to the door before his voice arrested her. "I . . . ah . . . I don't suppose," he said, "that you are familiar with Aubrey's *Brief Lives*, are you?"

"No," she said. "Who was *he* when he was at home?"

"He wrote a 'brief life' of a man called Sir Jonas Moore. It begins: 'Sciatica he cured it, by boyling his buttocks.' I'm glad, at least, you don't propose to try that remedy."

"Well!" cried Nurse Kettle delightedly. "You *are* coming out of your shell, to be sure. Nighty-bye."

3

During the next three days Nurse Kettle, pedalling about her duties, had occasion to notice, and she was sharp in such matters, that something untoward was going on in the district. Wherever she went, whether it was to attend upon Lady Lacklander's toe, or upon the abscess of the gardener's child at Hammer, or upon Commander Syce's strangely persistent lumbago, she felt a kind of heightened tension in the behaviour of her patients and also in the behaviour of young Dr. Mark Lacklander. Rose Cartarette, when she encountered her in the garden, was white and jumpy; the Colonel looked strained and Mrs. Cartarette singularly excited.

"Kettle," Lady Lacklander said, on Wednesday, wincing a little as she endured the approach of a fomentation to her toe, "have you got the cure for a bad conscience?"

Nurse Kettle did not resent being addressed in this restoration-comedy fashion by Lady Lacklander, who had known her for some twenty years and used the form with an intimate and even an affectionate air much prized by Nurse Kettle.

"Ah," said the latter, "there's no mixture-as-before for *that* sort of trouble."

"No. How long." Lady Lacklander went on, "have you been looking after us in Swevenings, Kettle?"

"Thirty years if you count five in the hospital at Chyning."

"Twenty-five years of fomentations, enemas, slappings, and thumpings," mused Lady Lacklander. "And I suppose you've learnt quite a lot about us in that time. There's nothing like illness to reveal character and there's nothing like a love affair," she added unexpectedly, "to disguise it. This is agony," she ended mildly, referring to the fomentation.

"Stick it if you can, dear," Nurse Kettle advised, and Lady Lacklander for her part did not object to being addressed as "dear" by Nurse Kettle, who continued, "How do you mean, I wonder, about love disguising character?"

"When people are in love," Lady Lacklander said

with a little scream as a new fomentation was applied, "they instinctively present themselves to each other in their most favourable light. They assume pleasing characteristics as unconsciously as a cock pheasant puts on his spring plumage. They display such virtues as magnanimity, charitableness and modesty and wait for them to be admired. They develop a positive genius for suppressing their least attractive points. They can't help it, you know, Kettle. It's just the behaviourism of courtship."

"Fancy."

"Now don't pretend you don't know what I'm talking about, because you most certainly do. You think straight and that's more than anybody else seems to be capable of doing in Swevenings. You're a gossip, of course," Lady Lacklander added, "but I don't think you're a malicious gossip, are you?"

"Certainly not. The idea!"

"No. Tell me, now, without any frills, what do you think of *us?*"

"Meaning, I take it," Nurse Kettle returned, "the aristocracy?"

"Meaning exactly that. Do you," asked Lady Lacklander with relish, "find us effete, ineffectual, vicious, obsolete and altogether extraneous?"

"No," said Nurse Kettle stoutly, "I don't."

"Some of are, you know."

Nurse Kettle squatted back on her haunches retaining a firm grip on Lady Lacklander's little heel. "It's not the people so much as the idea," she said.

"Ah," said Lady Lacklander, "you're an Elizabethan, Kettle. You *believe* in degree. You're a female Ulysses, old girl. But degree is now dependent upon behaviour, I'd have you know."

Nurse Kettle gave a jolly laugh and said she didn't know what that meant. Lady Lacklander rejoined that, among other things, it meant that if people fall below something called a certain standard, they are asking for trouble. "I mean," Lady Lacklander went on, scowling with physical pain and mental concentration, "I mean we'd better behave ourselves in the admittedly few jobs that by right of heritage used to be ours. I mean, finally, that whether they think we're rubbish or whether they think we're not, people still expect that in certain situations we will give certain reactions. Don't they, Kettle?"

Nurse Kettle said she supposed they did.

"Not," Lady Lacklander said, "that I give a damn what they think. But still . . ."

She remained wrapped in moody contemplation while Nurse Kettle completed her treatment and bandaged the toe.

"In short," her formidable patient at last delcaimed, "we can allow ourselves to be almost anything but shabbily behaved. That we'd better avoid. I'm extremely worried, Kettle." Nurse Kettle looked up enquiringly. "Tell me, is there any gossip in the village about my grandson? Romantic gossip?"

"A bit," Nurse Kettle said and after a pause added, "It'd be lovely, wouldn't it? She's a sweet girl. *And* an heiress into the bargain."

"Umph."

"Which is not to be sneezed at nowadays, I suppose. They tell me everything goes to the daughter."

"Entailed," Lady Lacklander said. "Mark, of course, gets nothing until he succeeds. But it's not that that bothers me."

"Whatever it is, if I were you, I should consult Dr.

Mark, Lady Lacklander. An old head on young shoulders if ever I saw one."

"My dear soul, my grandson is, as you have observed, in love. He is, therefore, as I have tried to point out, extremely likely to take up a high-falutin' attitude. Besides, he's involved. No, I must take matters into my own hands, Kettle. Into my own hands. You go past Hammer on your way home, don't you?"

Nurse Kettle said she did.

"I've written a note to Colonel Cartarette. Drop it there like a good creature, will you?"

Nurse Kettle said she would and fetched it from Lady Lacklander's writing desk.

"It's a pity," Lady Lacklander muttered, as Nurse Kettle was about to leave. "It's a pity poor George is such an ass."

4

She considered that George gave only too clear a demonstration of being an ass when she caught a glimpse of him on the following evening. He was playing a round of golf with Mrs. Cartarette. George, having attained the tricky age for Lacklanders, had fallen into a muddled, excited dotage upon Kitty Cartarette. She made him feel dangerous, and this sensation enchanted him. She told him repeatedly how chivalrous he was and so cast a glow of knight-errantry over impulses that are not usually seen in that light. She allowed him only the most meagre rewards, doling out the lesser stimulants of courtship in positively homeopathic doses. Thus on the Nunspardon golf course, he was allowed to watch, criticize and correct her swing. If his interest in this exercise was far from being purely athletic, Mrs. Cartarette gave only the slightest hint that she was aware of the fact and industriously swung and swung again while he fell back to observe, and advanced to adjust, her technique.

Lady Lacklander, tramping down River Path in the cool of the evening with a footman in attendance to carry her sketching impedimenta and her shooting-stick, observed her son and his pupil as it were in pantomime on the second tee. She noticed how George rocked on his feet, with his head on one side, while Mrs. Cartarette swung, as Lady Lacklander angrily noticed, everything that a woman could swing. Lady Lacklander looked at the two figures with distaste tempered by speculation. "Can George," she wondered, "have some notion of employing the strategy of indirect attack upon Maurice? But no, poor boy, he hasn't got the brains."

The two figures disappeared over the crest of the hill, and Lady Lacklander plodded heavily on in great distress of mind. Because of her ulcerated toe she wore a pair of her late husband's shooting boots. On her head was a battered solar topee of immense antiquity which she found convenient as an eye-shade. For the rest, her vast person was clad in baggy tweeds and a tent-like blouse. Her hands, as always, were encrusted with diamonds.

She and the footman reached Bottom Bridge, turned left and came to a halt before a group of elders and the prospect of a bend in the stream. The footman, under Lady Lacklander's direction, set up her easel, filled her water-jar at the stream, placed her camp stool and put her shooting-stick beside it. When she fell back from her work in order to observe it as a whole, Lady Lacklander was in the habit of supporting her bulk upon the shooting-stick.

The footman left her. She would reappear in her own time at Nunspardon and change for dinner at nine o'clock. The footman would return and collect her impedimenta. She fixed her spectacles on her nose, directed at her subject the sort of glance Nurse Kettle often bestowed on a recalcitrant patient, and set to work, massive and purposeful before her easel.

It was at half past six that she established herself there, in the meadow on the left bank of the Chyne not far below Bottom Bridge.

At seven, Mr. Danberry-Phinn, having assembled his paraphernalia for fishing, set off down Watt's Hill. He did not continue to Bottom Bridge but turned left, and made for the upper reaches of the Chyne.

At seven, Mark Lacklander, having looked in on a patient in the village, set off on foot along Watt's lane. He carried his case of instruments, as he wished to lance the abscess of the gardener's child at Hammer, and his racket and shoes, as he proposed to play tennis with Rose Cartarette. He also hoped to have an extremely serious talk with her father.

At seven, Nurse Kettle, having delivered Lady Lacklander's note at Hammer, turned in at Commander Syce's drive and free-wheeled to his front door.

At seven, Sir George Lacklander, finding himself favourably situated in a sheltered position behind a group of trees, embraced Mrs. Cartarette with determination, fervour and an ulterior motive.

It was at this hour that the hopes, passions and fears that had slowly mounted in intensity since the death of Sir Harold Lacklander began to gather an emotional

68

momentum and slide towards each other like so many downhill streams, influenced in their courses by accidents and detail, but destined for a common and profound agitation.

At Hammer, Rose and her father sat in his study and gazed at each other in dismay.

"When did Mark tell you?" Colonel Cartarette asked.

"On that same night . . . after you came in and . . . and found us. He went to Nunspardon and his father told him and then he came back here and told me. Of course," Rose said looking at her father with eyes as blue as periwinkles behind their black lashes, "of course it wouldn't have been any good for Mark to pretend nothing had happened. It's quite extraordinary how each of us seems to know exactly what the other one's thinking."

The Colonel leant his head on his hand and half smiled at this expression of what he regarded as one of the major fallacies of love. "My poor darling," he murmured.

"Daddy, you do understand, don't you, that theoretically Mark is absolutely on your side? Because . . . well, because the facts of any case always should be demonstrated. I mean, that's the scientific point of view."

The Colonel's half-smile twisted, but he said nothing.

"And I agree, too, absolutely," Rose said, "other things being equal."

"Ah!" said the Colonel.

"But they're not, darling," Rose cried out, "they're nothing like equal. In terms of human happiness, they're all cockeyed. Mark says his grandmother's so desperately worried that with all this coming on top of Sir Harold's death and everything she may crack up altogether."

The Colonel's study commanded a view of his own spinney and of that part of the valley that the spinney did not mask: Bottom Bridge and a small area below it on the right bank of the Chyne. Rose went to the window and looked down. "She's down there somewhere," she said, "sketching in Bottom Meadow on the far side. She only sketches when she's fussed."

"She's sent me a chit. She wants me to go down and talk to her at eight o'clock when I suppose she'll have done a sketch and hopes to feel less fussed. Damned inconvenient hour but there you are. I'll cut dinner, darling, and try the evening rise. Ask them to leave supper for me, will you, and apologies to Kitty."

"O.K.," Rose said with forced airiness. "And, of course," she added, "there's the further difficulty of Mark's papa."

"George."

"Yes, indeed, George. Well, we know he's not exactly as bright as sixpence, don't we, but all the same he *is* Mark's papa, and he's cutting up most awfully rough and . . ."

Rose caught back her breath, her lips trembled, and her eyes filled with tears. She launched herself into her father's arms and burst into a flood of tears. "What's the use," poor Rose sobbed, "of being a brave little woman? I'm not in the least brave. When Mark asked me to marry him, I said I wouldn't because of you and there I was, so miserable that when he asked me again I said I would. And now, when we're so desperately in love, this happens. We have to do them this really

70

frightful injury. Mark says of course they must take it and it won't make any difference to *us*, but of course it *will*, and how can I bear to be married to Mark and know how his people feel about you when next to Mark, my darling, darling Daddy, I love you best in the world? And *his* father," Rose wept, "*his* father says that if Mark marries me, he'll never forgive him and that they'll do a sort of Montague and Capulet thing to us and, darling, it wouldn't be much fun for Mark and me, would it, to be star-crossed lovers?"

"My poor baby," murmured the agitated and sentimental Colonel, "my poor baby!" And he administered a number of unintentionally hard thumps between his daughter's shoulder blades.

"It's so many people's happiness," Rose sobbed. "It's all of us."

Her father dabbed at her eyes with his own handkerchief, kissed her and put her aside. In his turn he went over to the window and looked down at Bottom Bridge and up at the roofs of Nunspardon. There were no figures in view on the golf course.

"You know, Rose," the Colonel said in a changed voice, "I don't carry the whole responsibility. There is a final decision to be made, and mine must rest upon it. Don't hold out too many hopes, my darling, but I suppose there is a chance. I've time to get it over before I talk to Lady Lacklander, and indeed I suppose I should. There's nothing to be gained by any further delay. I'll go now."

He went to his desk, unlocked a drawer and took out an envelope.

Rose said, "Does Kitty . . . ?"

"Oh, yes," the Colonel said. "She knows."

"Did you tell her, Daddy?"

The Colonel had already gone to the door. Without turning his head and with an air too casual to be convincing, he said, "O, no. No. She arranged to play a round of golf with George, and I imagine he elected to tell her. He's a fearful old gas-bag is George."

"She's playing now, isn't she?"

"Is she? Yes," said the Colonel, "I believe she is. He came to fetch her, I think. It's good for her to get out."

"Yes, rather," Rose agreed.

Her father went out to call on Mr. Octavius Danberry-Phinn. He took his fishing gear with him as he intended to go straight on to his meeting with Lady Lacklander and to ease his troubled mind afterwards with the evening rise. He also took his spaniel Skip, who was trained to good behaviour when he accompanied his master to the trout stream.

5

Lady Lacklander consulted the diamond-encrusted watch which was pinned to her tremendous bosom and discovered that it was now seven o'clock. She had been painting for half an hour and an all-too-familiar phenomenon had emerged from her efforts.

"It's a curious thing," she meditated, "that a woman of my character and determination should produce such a puny affair. However, it's got me in better trim for Maurice Cartarette, and that's a damn' good thing. An hour to go if he's punctual, and he's sure to be that."

She tilted her sketch and ran a faint green wash over the foreground. When it was partly dry, she rose from her stool, tramped some distance away to the crest of a hillock, seated herself on her shooting-stick and contemplated her work through a lorgnette tricked out with diamonds. The shooting-stick sank beneath her in the soft meadowland so that the disk which was designed to check its descent was itself imbedded to the depth of several inches. When Lady Lacklander returned to her easel, she merely abandoned her shooting-stick, which remained in a vertical position and from a distance looked a little like a giant fungoid growth. Sticking up above intervening hillocks and rushes, it was observed over the top of his glasses by the longsighted Mr. Phinn when, accompanied by Thomasina Twitchett, he came nearer to Bottom Bridge. Keeping on the right bank, he began to cast his fly in a somewhat mannered but adroit fashion over the waters most often frequented by the Old 'Un. Lady Lacklander, whose ears were as sharp as his, heard the whirr of his reel and, remaining invisible, was perfectly able to deduce the identity and movements of the angler. At the same time, far above them on Watt's Hill, Colonel Cartarette, finding nobody but seven cats at home at Jacob's Cottage, walked round the house and looking down into the little valley at once spotted both Lady Lacklander and Mr. Phinn, like figures in Nurse Kettle's imaginary map, the one squatting on her camp stool, the other in slow motion near Bottom Bridge.

"I've time to speak to him before I see her," thought the Colonel. "But I'll leave it here in case we don't meet." He posted his long envelope in Mr. Phinn's front door, and then greatly troubled in spirit, he made for the river path and went down into the valley, the old spaniel, Skip, walking at his heels.

Nurse Kettle, looking through the drawing-room window at Uplands, caught sight of the Colonel before he disappeared beyond Commander Syce's spinney. She administered a final tattoo with the edges of her muscular hands on Commander Syce's lumbar muscles and said, "There goes the Colonel for the evening rise. You wouldn't have stood *that* amount of punishment two days ago, would you?"

"No," a submerged voice said, "I suppose not."

"Well! So that's all I get for my trouble."

"No, no! Look here, look here!" he gabbled, twisting his head in an attempt to see her. "Good heavens! What are you saying?"

"All right. I know. I was only pulling your leg. There!" she said. "That's all for to-day and I fancy it won't be long before I wash my hands of you altogether."

"Of course I can't expect to impose on your kindness any longer."

Nurse Kettle was clearing up. She appeared not to hear this remark and presently bustled away to wash her hands. When she returned, Syce was sitting on the edge of his improvised bed. He wore slacks, a shirt, a scarf and a dressing gown.

"Jolly D.," said Nurse Kettle. "Done it all yourself."

"I hope you will give me the pleasure of joining me for a drink before you go.'"

"On duty?"

"Isn't it off duty, now?"

"Well," said Nurse Kettle, "I'll have a drink with you, but I hope it won't mean that when I've gone on me way rejoicing, you're going to have half a dozen more with yourself."

Commander Syce turned red and muttered something about a fellah having nothing better to do.

"Get along," said Nurse Kettle, "find something better. The idea!"

They had their drinks, looking at each other with an air of comradeship. Commander Syce, using a walking-stick and holding himself at an unusual angle, got out an album of photographs taken when he was on the active list in the navy. Nurse Kettle adored photographs and was genuinely interested in a long sequence of naval vessels, odd groups of officers and views of seaports. Presently she turned a page and discovered quite a dashing water-colour of a corvette and then an illustrated menu with lively little caricatures in the margin. These she greatly admired and observing a terrified and defiant expression on the face of her host, ejaculated, "You never did these yourself! You *did!* Well, aren't you the clever one!"

Without answering, he produced a small portfolio, which he silently thrust at her. It contained many more sketches. Although Nurse Kettle knew nothing about pictures, she did, she maintained, know what she liked. And she liked these very much indeed. They were direct statements of facts, and she awarded them direct statements of approval and was about to shut the portfolio when a sketch that had faced the wrong way round caught her attention. She turned it over. It was of a woman lying on a chaise-longue smoking a cigarette in a jade holder. A bougainvillea flowered in the background.

"Why," Nurse Kettle ejaculated. "Why, that's Mrs. Cartarette!"

If Syce had made some kind of movement to snatch the sketch from her, he checked himself before it was completed. He said very rapidly, "Party. Met her Far

East. Shore Leave. Forgotten all about it."

"That would be before they were married, wouldn't it?" Nurse Kettle remarked with perfect simplicity. She shut the portfolio, said, "You know I believe you could make my picture-map of Swevenings," and told him of her great desire for one. When she got up and collected her belongings, he too rose, but with an ejaculation of distress.

"I see I haven't made a job of you yet," she remarked. "Same time to-morrow suit you?"

"Admirably," he said. "Thank you, thank you, thank you." He gave her one of his rare painful smiles and watched her as she walked down the path towards his spinney. It was now a quarter to nine.

Nurse Kettle had left her bicycle in the village, where she was spending the evening with the Women's Institute. She therefore took the river path. Dusk had fallen over the valley of the Chyne, and as she descended into it, her own footfall sounded unnaturally loud on the firm turf. Thump, thump, thump she went, down the hillside. Once, she stopped dead, tilted her head and listened. From behind her at Uplands came the not unfamiliar sound of a twang followed by a sharp penetrating blow. She smiled to herself and walked on. Only desultory rural sounds disturbed the quiet of nightfall. She could actually hear the cool voice of the stream.

She did not cross Bottom Bridge but followed a rough path along the right bank of the Chyne, past a group of elders and another of willows. This second group, extending in a sickle-shaped mass from the water's edge into Bottom Meadow, rose up vapourishly in the dusk. She could smell willow leaves and wet soil. As sometimes happens when we are

76

solitary, she had the sensation of being observed, but she was not a fanciful woman and soon dismissed this feeling.

"It's turned much cooler," she thought.

A cry of mourning, intolerably loud, rose from beyond the willows and hung on the night air. A thrush whirred out of the thicket close to her face, and the cry broke and wavered again. It was the howl of a dog.

She pushed through the thicket into an opening by the river and found the body of Colonel Cartarette with his spaniel Skip beside it, mourning him.

CHAPTER IV

Bottom Meadow

Nurse Kettle was acquainted with death. She did not need Skip's lament to tell her that the curled figure resting its head on a turf of river grass was dead. She knelt beside it and pushed her hand under the tweed jacket and silk shirt. "Cooling," she thought. A tweed hat with fisherman's flies in the band lay over the face. Someone, she thought, might almost have dropped it here. She lifted it and remained quite still with it suspended in her hand. The Colonel's temple had been broken as if his head had come under a waxworker's hammer. The spaniel threw back his head and howled again.

"O, do be quiet!" Nurse Kettle ejaculated. She replaced the hat and stood up, knocking her head against a branch. The birds that spent the night in the willows stirred again and some of them flew out with a sharp whirring sound. The Chyne gurgled and plopped and somewhere up in Nunspardon woods an owl hooted. "He has been murdered," thought Nurse Kettle.

Through her mind hurtled all the axioms of police procedure as laid down in her chosen form of escape-literature. One must, she recollected, not touch the body, and she had touched it. One must send at once for the police, but she had nobody to send. She thought there was also something about not leaving the body, yet to telephone or to fetch Mr. Oliphant, the police-sergeant at Chyning, she would have to leave the body, and while she was away, the spaniel, she supposed, would sit beside it and howl. It was now quite darkish and the moon not yet up. She could see, however, not far from the Colonel's hands, the glint of a trout's scales in the grass and of a knife blade nearby. His rod was laid out on the lip of the bank, less than a pace from where he lay. None of these things, of course, must be disturbed. Suddenly Nurse Kettle thought of Commander Syce, whose Christian name she had discovered was Geoffrey, and wished with all her heart that he was at hand to advise her. The discovery in herself of this impulse astonished her and, in a sort of flurry, she swapped Geoffrey Syce for Mark Lacklander. "I'll find the doctor," she thought.

She patted Skip. He whimpered and scratched at her knees with his paws. "Don't howl, doggy," she said in a trembling voice. "Good boy! Don't howl." She took up her bag and turned away.

As she made her way out of the willow grove, she wondered for the first time about the identity of the being who had reduced Colonel Cartarette to the status of a broken waxwork. A twig snapped. "Suppose," she thought, "he's still about! Help, what a notion!" And as she hurried back along the path to Bottom Bridge, she tried not to think of the dense shadows and dark hollows that lay about her. Up on Watt's Hill the three houses—Jacob's Cottage, Uplands and Hammer—all had lighted windows and drawn blinds. They looked very far off to Nurse Kettle.

She crossed Bottom Bridge and climbed the zigzag path that skirted the golf course, coming finally to the Nunspardon Home Spinney. Only now did she remember that her flashlamp was in her bag. She got it out and found that she was breathless. "Too quick up the hill," she thought. "Keep your shirt on, Kettle." River Path proper ran past the spinney to the main road, but a by-path led up through the trees into the grounds of Nunspardon. This she took and presently came out into the open gardens with the impressive Georgian facade straight ahead of her.

The footman who answered the front door bell was well enough known to her. "Yes, it's me again, William," she said. "Is the doctor at home?"

"He came in about an hour ago, miss."

"I want to see him. It's urgent."

"The family's in the library, miss. I'll ascertain . . ."

"Don't bother," said Nurse Kettle. "Or, yes. Ascertain if you like, but I'll be hard on your heels. Ask him if he'll come out here and speak to me."

He looked dubiously at her, but something in her face must have impressed him. He crossed the great hall and opened the library door. He left it open and Nurse Kettle heard him say, "Miss Kettle to see Dr. Lacklander, my lady."

"Me?" said Mark's voice. "O Lord! All right, I'll come."

"Bring her in here," Lady Lacklander's voice commanded. "Talk to her in here, Mark. I want to see Kettle." Hearing this, Nurse Kettle, without waiting to be summoned, walked quickly into the library. The three Lacklanders had turned in their chairs. George and

Mark got up. Mark looked sharply at her and came quickly towards her. Lady Lacklander said, "Kettle! What's happened to *you!*"

Nurse Kettle said, "Good evening, Lady Lacklander. Good evening, Sir George." She put her hands behind her back and looked full at Mark. "May I speak to you, sir?" she said. "There's been an accident."

"All right, Nurse," Mark said. "To whom?"

"To Colonel Cartarette, sir."

The expression of enquiry seemed to freeze on their faces. It was as if they retired behind newly assumed masks.

"What sort of accident?" Mark said.

He stood behind Nurse Kettle and his grandmother and father. She shaped the word "killed" with her lips and tongue.

"Come out here," he muttered and took her by the arm.

"Not at all," his grandmother said. She heaved herself out of her chair and bore down upon them. "Not at all, Mark. What has happened to Maurice Cartarette? Don't keep things from me; I am probably in better trim to meet an emergency than anyone else in this house. What has happened to Maurice?"

Mark, still holding Nurse Kettle by the arm, said, "Very well, Gar. Nurse Kettle will tell us what has happened."

"Let's have it, then. And in case it's as bad as you look, Kettle, I suggest we all sit down. What did you say, George?"

Her son had made an indeterminate noise. He now said galvanically, "Yes, of course, Mama, by all means."

Mark pushed a chair forward for Nurse Kettle, and she took it thankfully. Her knees, she discovered, were wobbling.

"Now, then, out with it," said Lady Lacklander. "He's dead, isn't he, Kettle?"

"Yes, Lacy Lacklander."

"Where?" Sir George demanded. Nurse Kettle told him.

"When," Lady Lacklander said, "did you discover him?"

"I've come straight up here, Lady Lacklander."

"But why here, Kettle? Why not to Uplands?"

"I must break it to Kitty," said George.

"I must go to Rose," said Mark simultaneously.

"Kettle," said Lady Lacklander, "you used the word accident. What accident?"

"He has been murdered, Lady Lacklander," said Nurse Kettle.

The thought that crossed her mind after she had made this announcement was that the three Lack-landers were, in their several generations, superficially very much alike but that whereas in Lady Lacklander and Mark the distance between the eyes and the width of mouth suggested a certain generosity, in Sir George they seemed merely to denote the naive. Sir George's jaw dropped, and handsome though he undoubtedly was, he gaped unhandsomely. As none of them spoke, she added, "So I thought I'd better report to you, sir."

"Do you mean," Sir George said loudly, "that he's lying there in my bottom meadow, murdered?"

"Yes, Sir George," Nurse Kettle said, "I do."

"How?" Mark said.

"Injuries to the head."

"You made quite sure, of course?"

"Quite sure."

Mark looked at his father. "We must ring the Chief Constable," he said. "Would you do that, Father? I'll go down with Nurse Kettle. One of us had better stay there till the police come. If you can't get the C.C., would you ring Sergeant Oliphant at Chyning?"

Sir George's hand went to his moustache. "I think," he said, "you may take it, Mark, that I understand my responsibilities."

Lady Lacklander said, "Don't be an ass, George. The boy's quite right," and her son, scarlet in the face, went off to the telephone. "Now," Lady Lacklander continued, "what are we going to do about Rose and that wife of his?"

"Gar . . ." Mark began, but his grandmother raised a fat glittering hand.

"Yes, yes," she said. "No doubt you want to break it to Rose, Mark, but in my opinion you will do better to let me see both of them first. I shall stay there until you appear. Order the car."

Mark rang the bell. "And you needn't wait," she added. "Take Miss Kettle with you." It was characteristic of Lady Lacklander that she restricted her use of the more peremptory form of address to the second person. She now used it. "Kettle," she said, "we're grateful to you and mustn't impose. Would you rather come with me or go back with my grandson. Which is best, do you think?"

"I'll go with the doctor, thank you, Lady Lacklander. I suppose," Nurse Kettle added composedly, "that as I found the body, I'll be required to make a statement."

She had moved with Mark to the door when Lady

Lacklander's voice checked her.

"And I suppose," the elderly voice said, "that as I may have been the last person to speak to him, I shall be required to make one, too."

2

In the drawing-room at Hammer there was an incongruous company assembled. Kitty Cartarette, Mark Lacklander and Nurse Kettle waited there while Lady Lacklander sat with Rose in the Colonel's study. She had arrived first at Hammer, having been driven round in her great car while Mark and Nurse Kettle waited in the valley and George rang up the police station at Chyning. George had remembered he was a Justice of the Peace and was believed to be in telephonic conference with his brethren of the bench.

So it had fallen to Lady Lacklander to break the news to Kitty, whom she had found, wearing her black-velvet tights and flame-coloured top, in the drawing-room. Lady Lacklander in the course of a long life spent in many embassies had encountered every kind of eccentricity in female attire and was pretty well informed as to the predatory tactics of women whom, in the Far East, she had been wont to describe as "light cruisers." She had made up her mind about Kitty Cartarette but had seemed to be prepared to concede her certain qualities if she showed any signs of possessing them.

She had said, "My dear, I'm the bearer of bad tidings," and noticing that Kitty at once looked very frightened, had remarked to herself, "She thinks I mean to tackle her about George."

"Are you?" Kitty had said. "What sort of tidings, please?"

"About Maurice." Lady Lacklander had waited for a moment, added, "I'm afraid it's the worst kind of news," and had then told her. Kitty stared at her. "Dead?" she said. "Maurice dead? I don't believe you. How can he be dead? He's been fishing down below there and I daresay he's looked in at the pub." Her hands with their long painted nails began to tremble. "How can he be dead?" she repeated.

Lady Lacklander became more specific, and presently Kitty broke into a harsh strangulated sobbing, twisting her fingers together and turning her head aside. She walked about the room, still, Lady Lacklander noticed, swaying her hips. Presently she fetched up by a grog tray on a small table and shakily poured herself a drink.

"That's a sensible idea," Lady Lacklander said as the neck of the decanter chattered against the glass. Kitty awkwardly offered her a drink, which she declined with perfect equanimity. "Her manner," she thought to herself, "is really too dreadful. What shall I do if George marries her?"

It was at this juncture that Nurse Kettle and Mark had appeared outside the French windows. Lady Lacklander signalled to them. "Here are my grandson and Nurse Kettle," she said to Kitty. "Shall they come in? I think it would be a good idea, don't you?"

Kitty said shakily, "Yes, please. Yes, if you like." Lady Lacklander heaved her bulk out of her chair and let them in.

"Sergeant Oliphant's there," Mark murmured. "They're going to ring Scotland Yard. Does Rose . . . ?"

"Not yet. She's out in the garden, somewhere."

Mark went across to Kitty and spoke to her with a quiet authority that his grandmother instantly approved. She noticed how Kitty steadied under it, how Mark, without fussing, got her into a chair. Nurse Kettle, as a matter of course, came forward and took the glass when Kitty had emptied it. A light and charming voice sang in the hall:

"Come away, come away, death . . ." and Mark turned sharply.

"I'll go," his grandmother said, "and I'll fetch you when she asks for you."

With a swifter movement than either her size or her age would have seemed to allow she had gone into the hall. The little song of death stopped, and the door shut behind Lady Lacklander.

Kitty Cartarette was quieter but still caught her breath now and again in a harsh sob.

"Sorry," she said looking from Nurse Kettle to Mark. "Thanks. It's just the shock."

"Yes, of course, dear," Nurse Kettle said.

"I sort of can't believe it. You know?"

"Yes, of course," Mark said.

"It seems so queer . . . Maurice!" She looked at Mark. "What was that," she said, "about somebody doing it? Is it true?"

"I'm afraid it looks very much like it."

"I'd forgotten," she muttered vaguely. "You've seen him, haven't you, and you're a doctor, of course." Her mouth trembled. She wiped the back of her hand over it. A trail of red was dragged across her cheek. It was a sufficient indication of her state of mind that she seemed to be unaware of it. She said, "No, it's no good, I can't believe it. We saw him down there, fishing." And then she suddenly demanded, "Where George?"

Nurse Kettle saw Mark's back stiffen. "My father?" he asked.

"O, yes, of course, I'd forgotten," she said again, shaking her head. "He's your father. Silly of me."

"He's looking after one or two things that must be done. You see, the police have had to be told at once."

"Is George getting the police?"

"He's rung them up. He will, I think, come here as soon as he can."

"Yes," she said. "I expect he will."

Nurse Kettle saw George's son compress his lips. At that moment George himself walked in and the party became even less happily assorted.

Nurse Kettle had acquired a talent for retiring into whatever background presented itself, and this talent she now exercised. She moved through the open French window onto the terrace, shut the door after her and sat on a garden seat within view of the drawing-room but facing across the now completely dark valley. Mark, who would perhaps have liked to follow her, stood his ground. His father, looking extraordinarily handsome and not a little self-conscious, went straight to Kitty. She used the gesture that Mark had found embarrassing and extended her left hand to Sir George, who kissed it with an air nicely compounded of embarrassment, deference, distress and devotion.

"My dear Kitty," said Sir George in a special voice, "I'm so terribly, terribly sorry. What can one say! What can one do!"

He apparently had already said and done more than any of the others to assuage Kitty's distress, for it began perceptibly to take on a more becoming guise. She looked into his eyes and said, "How terribly good of you to come." He sat down beside her, began to pat her hand, noticed his son and said, "I'll have a word with you in a moment, old boy."

Mark was about to retire to the terrace when the door opened and his grandmother looked in. "Mark?" she said. He went quickly into the hall. "In the study," Lady Lacklander said, and in a moment he was there with Rose sobbing bitterly in his arms.

"You need pay no attention to me," Lady Lacklander said. "I am about to telephone New Scotland Yard. Your father tells me they have been called in, and I propose to send for Helena Alleyn's boy."

Mark, who was kissing Rose's hair, left off abruptly to say, "Can you mean Chief Inspector Alleyn, Gar?"

"I don't know what his rank is, but he used to be a nice boy twenty-five years ago before he left the Service to become a constable. Central? This is Hermione, Lady Lacklander. I want New Scotland Yard, London. The call is extremely urgent as it is concerned with murder. Yes, murder. You will oblige me by putting it through at once. Thank you." She glanced at Mark. "In the circumstances," she said, "I prefer to deal with a gent."

Mark had drawn Rose to a chair and was kneeling beside her, gently wiping away her tears.

"Hullo!" Lady Lacklander said after an extremely short delay. "New Scotland Yard. This is Hermione, Lady Lacklander, speaking. I wish to speak to Mr. Roderick Alleyn. If he is not on your premises, you will no doubt know where he is to be found. I don't know his rank . . ."

89

Her voice, aristocratic, cool, sure of itself, went steadily on. Mark dabbed at Rose's eyes. His father, alone with Kitty in the drawing-room, muttered agitatedly, " . . . I'm sorry it's hit you so hard, Kit."

Kitty looked wanly at him. "I suppose it's the shock," she said, and added without rancour, "I'm not as tough as you all think." He protested chaotically. "O," she said quite gently, "I know what they'll say about me. Not you, p'raps, but the others. They'll say it's cupboard-sorrow. 'That's what's upsetting the widow,' they'll say. I'm the outsider, George."

"Don't, Kit. Kit, listen . . ." He began to plead with her. "There's something I must ask you—if you'd just have a look for—you know—that thing—I mean—if it was found—"

She listened to him distractedly. "It's awful," George said. "I know it's awful to talk like this now, Kitty, but all the same—all the same—with so much at stake. I know you'll understand." Kitty said, "Yes. All right. Yes. But let me *think*."

Nurse Kettle out on the terrace was disturbed by the spatter of a few giant rain drops.

"There's going to be a storm," she said to herself. "A summer storm."

And since she would have been out of place in the drawing-room and in the study, she took shelter in the hall. She had no sooner done so than the storm broke in a downpour over the valley of the Chyne.

3

Alleyn and Fox had worked late, tidying up the last phase of a tedious case of embezzlement. At twelve minutes to ten they had finished. Alleyn shut the file with a slap of his hand.

"Dreary fellow," he said. "I hope they give him the maximum. Damn' good riddance. Come back with me and have a drink, Br'er Fox. I'm a grass-widower and hating it. Troy and Ricky are in the country. What do you say?"

Fox drew his hand across the lower part of his face. "Well, now, Mr. Alleyn, that sounds very pleasant," he said. "I say yes and thank you."

"Good." Alleyn looked round the familiar walls of the Chief Inspector's room at New Scotland Yard. "There are occasions," he said, "when one suddenly sees one's natural habitat as if for the first time. It is a terrifying sensation. Come on. Let's go while the going's good."

They were half-way to the door when the telephone rang. Fox said, "Ah, hell!" without any particular animosity and went back to answer it.

"Chief Inspector's room," he said heavily. "Well, yes, he's here. Just." He listened for a moment, gazing blandly at his superior. "Say I'm dead," Alleyn suggested moodily. Fox laid his great palm over the receiver. "They make out it's a Lady Lacklander on call from somewhere called Swevenings," he said.

"Lady *Lacklander?* Good lord! That's old Sir Harold Lacklander's widow," Alleyn ejaculated. "What's up with her, I wonder."

"Chief Inspector Alleyn will take the call," Fox said and held out the receiver.

Alleyn sat on his desk and put the receiver to his ear. An incisive elderly voice was saying ". . . I don't know his rank and I don't know whether he's on your premises or not, but you'll be good enough if you please to find Mr. Roderick Alleyn for me. It is Hermione, Lady Lacklander, speaking. Is that New Scotland Yard and have you heard me? I wish to speak to . . ."

Alleyn announced himself cautiously into the receiver. "Indeed!" the voice rejoined. "Why on earth couldn't you say so in the first instance? Hermione Lacklander speaking. I won't waste time reminding you about myself. You're Helena Alleyn's boy and I want an assurance from you. A friend of mine has just been murdered," the voice continued, "and I hear the local police are calling in your people. I would greatly prefer you, personally, to take charge of the whole thing. That can be arranged, I imagine?"

Alleyn, controlling his astonishment, said, "I'm afraid only if the Assistant Commissioner happens to give me the job."

"Who's he?"

Alleyn told her.

"Put me through to him," the voice commanded.

A second telephone began to ring. Fox answered it and in a moment held up a warning hand.

"Will you wait one second, Lady Lacklander?" Alleyn asked. Her voice, however, went incisively on, and he stifled it against his chest. "What the hell is it, Fox?" he asked irritably.

"Central office, sir. Orders for Swevenings. Homicide."

"Blistered apes! Us?"

"Us," said Fox stolidly.

Alleyn spoke into his own receiver. "Lady Lacklander? I *am* taking this case, it appears."

"Glad to hear it," said Lady Lacklander. "I suggest

you look pretty sharp about it. Au revoir," she added with unexpected modishness, and rang off.

Fox, in the meantime, had noted down instructions. "I'll inform Mr. Alleyn," he was saying. "Yes, very good, I'll inform him. Thank you." He hung up his receiver. "It's a Colonel Cartarette," he said. "We go to a place called Chyning in Barfordshire, where the local sergeant will meet us. Matter of two hours. Everything's laid on down below."

Alleyn had already collected his hat, coat and professional case. Fox followed his example. They went out together through the never-sleeping corridors.

It was a still, hot night. Sheet-lightning played fretfully over the East End. The air smelt of petrol and dust. "Why don't we join the River Police?" Alleyn grumbled. "One long water carnival."

A car waited for them with detective-Sergeants Bailey and Thompson and their gear already on board. As they drove out of the Yard, Big Ben struck ten.

"That's a remarkable woman, Fox," Alleyn said. "She's got a brain like a turbine and a body like a tun. My mother, who has her share of guts, was always terrified of Hermione Lacklander."

"Is that so, Mr. Alleyn? Her husband died only the other day, didn't he?"

"That's right. A quarter of a century ago he was one of my great white chiefs in the D.S. Solemn chap . . . just missed being brilliant. She was a force to be reckoned with even then. What's she doing in this party? What's the story, by the way?"

"A Colonel Cartarette found dead with head injuries by a fishing-stream. The C.C. down there says they're all tied up with the Royal Visit at Siminster and are understaffed, anyway, so they've called us in."

"Who found him?"

"A district nurse. About an hour ago."

"Fancy," said Alleyn mildly, and after a pause, "I wonder just why that old lady has come plunging in after me."

"I daresay," Fox said with great simplicity, "she has a fancy for someone of her own class."

Alleyn replied absently, "Do you, now?" and it said something for their friendship that neither of them felt the smallest embarrassment. Alleyn continued to ruminate on the Lacklanders. "Before the war," he said, "the old boy was Charge d'Affaires at Zlomce. The Special Branch got involved for a time, I remember. There was a very nasty bit of leakage: a decoded message followed by the suicide of the chap concerned. He was said to have been in cahoots with known agents. I was with the Special Branch at that time and had quite a bit to do with it. Perhaps the dowager wishes to revive old memories or something. Or perhaps she merely runs the village of Swevenings, murdered colonels and all, with the same virtuosity she brought to her husband's public life. Do you know Swevenings, Br'er Fox?"

"Can't say I do, sir."

"I do. Troy did a week's painting there a summer or two ago. It's superficially pretty and fundamentally beautiful," Alleyn said. "Quaint as hell, but take a walk after dusk and you wouldn't be surprised at anything you met. It's one of the oldest in England. 'Swevenings,' meaning Dreams. There was some near-prehistoric set-to in the valley, I forget what, and another during Bolingbroke's rebellion and yet another in the Civil Wars. This Colonel's blood is not the first soldier's, by a long chalk, to be spilt at Swevenings."

"They *will* do it," Fox said cryptically and with resignation. For a long time they drove on in a silence broken at long intervals by the desultory conversation of old friends.

"We're running into a summer storm," Alleyn said presently. Giant drops appeared on the windscreen and were followed in seconds by a blinding downpour.

"Nice set-up for field-work," Fox grumbled.

"It may be local. Although . . . no, by gum, we're nearly there. This is Chyning. Chyning: meaning, I fancy, a yawn or yawning."

"Yawns and dreams," Fox said. "Funny sort of district! What language would that be, Mr. Alleyn?"

"Chaucerian English, only don't depend on me. The whole district is called the Vale of Traunce, or brown-study. It all sounds hellishly quaint, but that's how it goes. There's the blue lamp."

The air smelt fresher when they got out. Rain drummed on roofs and flagstones and cascaded down the sides of houses. Alleyn led the way into a typical county police-station and was greeted by a tall sandy-haired sergeant.

"Chief Inspector Alleyn, sir? Sergeant Oliphant. Very glad to see you, sir."

"Inspector Fox," Alleyn said, introducing him. There followed a solemn shaking of hands and a lament that has become increasingly common of late years in the police force. "We're that short of chaps in the county," Sergeant Oliphant said, "we don't know which way to turn if anything of this nature crops up. The Chief Constable said to me, "Can we do it, Oliphant? Suppose we call on Siminster, can we do it?

And look, Mr. Alleyn, I had to say no, we can't."

Fox said, "T'ch."

"Well, exactly, Mr. Fox," Oliphant said. "If you haven't got the chaps, it's no good blundering in, is it? I've left my one P.C. in charge of the body, and that reduces my staff to me. Shall we move off, Mr. Alleyn? You'll find it wettish."

Alleyn and Fox accompanied the sergeant in his car while Bailey, Thompson and the Yard driver followed their lead. On the way Sergeant Oliphant gave a business-like report. Sir George Lacklander had rung up Sir James Punston, the Chief Constable, who in turn had rung Oliphant at a quarter to nine. Oliphant and his constable had then gone to Bottom Meadow and had found Dr. Mark Lacklander, Nurse Kettle and the body of Colonel Cartarette. They had taken a brief statement from Nurse Kettle and asked her to remain handy. Dr. Lacklander, who, in Oliphant's presence, made a very brief examination of the body, had then gone to break the news to the relatives of the deceased, taking Nurse Kettle with him. The sergeant had returned to Chyning and reported to the Chief Constable, who decided to call in the Yard. The constable had remained on guard by the body with Colonel Cartarette's spaniel, the latter having strenuously resisted all attempts to remove him.

"Did you form any opinion at all, Oliphant?" Alleyn asked. This is the most tactful remark a C.I.D. man can make to a county officer, and Oliphant coruscated under its influence.

"Not to say opinion, sir," he said. "Not to say that. One thing I did make sure of was not to disturb anything. He's lying on a patch of shingle screened in by a half-circle of willows and cut off on the open side by

e stream. He's lying on his right side, kind of curled
up as if he'd been bowled over from a kneeling position, like. His hat was over his face. Nurse Kettle
moved it when she found him, and Dr. Lacklander
moved it again when he examined the wound which is
in the left temple. A dirty great puncture," the
sergeant continued, easing off his official manner a
point or two, "with what the doctor calls extensive
fractures all round it. Quite turned my chap's stomach,
drunks-in-charge and disorderly behaviour being the
full extent of his experience."

Alleyn and Fox having chuckled in the right place,
the sergeant continued. "No sign of the weapon, so far
as we could make out, flashing our torches round. I
was particular not to go hoofing over the ground.

"Admirable," said Alleyn.

"Well," said Sergeant Oliphant; "it's what we're
told, sir, isn't it?"

"Notice anything at all out of the way?" Alleyn
asked. The question was inspired more by kindliness
than curiosity, and the sergeant's reaction surprised
him. Oliphant brought his two freckled hams of hands
down on the driving-wheel and made a complicated
snorting noise. "Out of the way!" he shouted. "Ah, my
God, I'll say we did. Out of the way! Tell me, now, sir,
are you a fly-fisherman?"

"Only fair to middling to worse. I do when I get the
chance. Why?"

"Now listen," Sergeant Oliphant said, quite aban-
doning his official position. "There's a dirty great fish
in this Chyne here would turn your guts over for you.
Pounds if he's an ounce, he is. Old in cunning, he is,
wary and sullen and that lordly in his lurkings and
slinkings he'd break your heart. Sometimes he'll rise

97

like a monster," said Sergeant Oliphant, urging his c[?] up Watt's hill, "and snap, he's took it, though that's only three times. Once being the deceased's doing a matter of a fortnight ago, which he left his cast in his jaws, he being a mighty fighter. And once the late squire Sir Harold Lacklander, which he lost him through being, as the man himself frankly admitted, overzealous in the playing of him, and NOW," the sergeant shouted, "NOW, for the last and final cast, hooked, played and landed by the poor Colonel, sir, and lying there by his dead body, or I can't tell a five-pound trout from a stickleback. Well, if he had to die, he couldn't have had a more glorious end. The Colonel, I mean, Mr. Alleyn, not the Old 'Un," said Sergeant Oliphant.

They had followed Watt's Lane down into the valley and up the slope through blinding rain to the village. Oliphant pulled up at a spot opposite the Boy and Donkey. A figure in a mackintosh and tweed hat stood in the lighted doorway.

"The Chief Constable, sir," said Oliphant. "Sir James Punston. He said he'd drive over and meet you."

"I'll have a word with him, before we go on. Wait a moment."

Alleyn crossed the road and introduced himself. The Chief Constable was a weather-beaten, tough-looking man who had been a Chief Commissioner of Police in India.

"Thought I'd better come over," Sir James said, "and take a look at this show. Damn' bad show it is. Damn' nice fellow, Cartarette. Can't imagine who'd want to set about him, but no doubt you'll be able to tell us. I'll come down with you. Filthy night, isn't it?"

The Yard car had drawn up behind Oliphant's. Bailey, Thompson and the driver got out and unloaded their gear with the economic movements of long usage and a stubborn disregard of the rain. The two parties joined up and led by the Chief Constable climbed a stile and followed a rough path down a drenched hillside. Their torches flashed on rods of rain and dripping furze bushes.

"They call this River Path," the Chief Constable said. "It's a right-of-way through the Nunspardon estate and comes out at Bottom Bridge, which we have to cross. I hear the dowager rang you up."

"She did indeed," Alleyn said.

"Lucky they decided it was your pigeon anyway. She'd have raised hell if they hadn't."

"I don't see where she fits in."

"She doesn't in any ordinary sense of the phrase. She's merely taken it upon herself ever since she came to Nunspardon to run Chyning and Swevenings. For some reason they seem to like it. Survival of the feudal instinct, you might think. It does survive, you know, in isolated pockets. Swevenings is an isolated pocket and Hermione, Lady Lacklander, has got it pretty well where she wants it." Sir James continued in this local strain as they slid and squelched down the muddy hillside. He gave Alleyn an account of the Cartarette family and their neighbours with a particularly racy profile of Lady Lacklander herself.

"There's the local gossip for you," he said. "Everybody knows everybody and has done so for centuries. There have been no stockbroking overflows into Swevenings. The Lacklanders, the Phinns, the Syces and the Cartarettes have lived in their respective houses for a great many generations. They're all on terms of intimacy, except that of late years there's been, I fancy, a little coolness between the Lacklanders and old Occy Phinn. And now I come to think of it, I fancy Maurice Cartarette fell out with Phinn over fishing or something. But then old Occy is really a bit mad. Rows with everybody. Cartarette, on the other hand, was a very pleasant, nice chap. Oddly formal and devilishly polite, though, especially with people he didn't like or had fallen out with. Not that he was a quarrelsome chap. Far from it. I have heard, by the way," Sir James gossiped, "that there's been some sort of coolness between Cartarette and that ass George Lacklander. However! And after all that, here's the bridge."

As they crossed it, they could hear the sound of rain beating on the surface of the stream. On the far side their feet sank into mud. They turned left on the rough path. Alleyn's shoes filled with water and water poured off the brim of his hat.

"Hell of a thing to happen, this bloody rain," said the Chief Constable. "Ruin the terrain."

A wet branch of willow slapped Alleyn's face. On the hill to their right they could see the lighted windows of three houses. As they walked on, however, distant groups of trees intervened and the windows were shut off.

"Can the people up there see into the actual area?" Alleyn asked.

Sergeant Oliphant said, "No, sir. Their own trees as well as this belt of willows screen it. They can see the stretch on the far side above the bridge, and a wee way below it."

"That's Mr. Danberry-Phinn's preserve, isn't it?" asked the Chief Constable. "Above the bridge?"

"Mr. *Danberry*-Phinn?" Alleyn said, sharply.

"Mr. Octavius Danberry-Phinn, to give you the complete works. The 'Danberry' isn't insisted upon. He's the local eccentric I told you about. He lives in the top house up there. We don't have a village idiot in Swevenings; we have a bloody-minded old gentleman. It's more classy," said Sir James, acidly.

"Danberry-Phinn," Alleyn repeated. "Isn't there some connection there with the Lacklanders?"

Sir James said shortly, "Both Swevenings men, of course." His voice faded uncertainly as he floundered into a patch of reeds. Somewhere close at hand a dog howled dismally and a deep voice apostrophized it, "Ah, stow it, will you." A light bobbed up ahead of them.

"Here we are," Sir James said. "That you, Gripper?"

"Yes, sir," said the deep voice. The mackintosh cape of uniformed constable shone in the torchlight.

"Dog still at it seemingly," said the sergeant.

"That's right, Mr. Oliphant. I've got him tethered here." A torch flashed on Skip, tied by a handkerchief to a willow branch.

"Hullo, old fellow," Alleyn said.

They all waited for him to go through the thicket. The constable shoved back a dripping willow branch for him.

"You'll need to stoop a little, sir."

Alleyn pushed through the thicket. His torchlight darted about in the rain and settled almost at once on a glistening mound.

"We got some groundsheets down and covered him," the sergeant said, "when it looked like rain."

"Good."

"And we've covered up the area round the corpse best we could. Bricks and one or two planks from the old boatshed yonder. But I daresay the water's got under just the same."

Alleyn said, "Fair enough. We couldn't ask for better. I think before we go any nearer we'll get photographs. Come through, Bailey. Do the best you can. As it stands and then uncovered, with all the details you can get, in case it washes out before morning. By Jove, though, I believe it's lifting."

They all listened. The thicket was loud with the sound of dripping foliage, but the heavy drumming of rain had stopped, and by the time Bailey had set up his camera, a waxing moon had ridden out over the valley.

When Bailey had taken his last flash-photograph of the area and the covered body, he took away the ground sheet and photographed the body again from many angles, first with the tweed hat over the face and then without it. He put his camera close to Colonel Cartarette's face and it flashed out in the night with raised eyebrows and pursed lips. Only when all this had been done, did Alleyn, walking delicately, go closer, stoop over the head and shine his torch full on the wound.

"Sharp instrument?" said Fox.

"Yes," Alleyn said, "yes, a great puncture, certainly. But could a sharp instrument do all that, Br'er Fox? No use speculating till we know what it was." His torchlight moved away from the face and found a silver glint on a patch of grass near Colonel Cartarette's hands and almost on the brink of the stream. "And this is the Old 'Un?" he murmured.

The Chief Constable and Sergeant Oliphant both broke into excited sounds of confirmation. The light moved to the hands, lying close together. One of them was clenched about a wisp of green.

"Cut grass," Alleyn said. "He was going to wrap his trout in it. There's his knife, and there's the creel beside him."

"What we reckoned, sir," said the sergeant in agreement.

"Woundy great fish, isn't it?" said the Chief Constable, and there was an involuntary note of envy in his voice.

Alleyn said, "What was the surface like before it rained?"

"Well, sir," the sergeant volunteered, "as you see, it's partly gravel. There was nothing to see in the willows where the ground was dry as a chip. There was what we reckoned were the deceased's footprints on the bank where it was soft and where he'd been fishing and one or two on the earthy bits near where he fell, but I couldn't make out anything else and we didn't try, for fear of messing up what little there was."

"Quite right. Will it rain again before morning?"

The three local men moved back into the meadow and looked up at the sky.

"All over, I reckon, sir," said the sergeant.

"Set fine," said the deep-voiced constable.

"Clearing," said Sir James Punston.

"Cover everything up again, Sergeant, and set a watch till morning. Have we any tips of any sort about times? Anybody known to have come this way?"

"Nurse Kettle, sir, who found him. Young Dr. Lacklander came back with her to look at him, and *he*

103

says he came through the valley and over the bridge earlier in the evening. We haven't spoken to anyone else, sir."

"How deep," Alleyn asked, "is the stream just here?"

"About five foot," said Sergeant Oliphant.

"Really? And he lies on his right side roughly parallel with the stream and facing it. Not more than two feet from the brink. Head pointing down-stream, feet towards the bridge. The fish lies right on the brink by the strand of grass he was cutting to wrap it in. And the wound's in the left temple. I take it he was squatting on his heels within two feet of the brink and just about to bed his catch down in the grass. Now, if, as the heelmarks near his feet seem to indicate, he kneeled straight over into the position the body still holds, one of two things must have happened, wouldn't you say, Br'er Fox?"

"Either," Fox said stolidly, "he was coshed by a left-handed person standing behind him or by a right-handed person standing in front of him and at least three feet away."

"Which would place the assailant," said Alleyn, "about twelve inches out on the surface of the stream. Which is not as absurd as it sounds when you put it that way. All right. Let's move on. What comes next?"

The Chief Constable, who had listened to all this in silence, now said, "I gather there's a cry of possible witnesses waiting for you up at Hammer. That's Cartarette's house up here on Watt's Hill. If you'll forgive me, Alleyn, I won't go up with you. Serve no useful purpose. If you want me, I'm five miles away at Tourets. Anything I can do, delighted, but sure you'd rather be left in peace. I would in my day. By the way,

I've told them at the Boy and Donkey that you'll probably want beds for what's left of the night. You'll find a room at the head of the stairs. They'll give you an early breakfast if you leave a note. Good-night."

He was gone before Alleyn could thank him.

With the sergeant as guide, Alleyn and Fox prepared to set out for Hammer. Alleyn had succeeded in persuading the spaniel Skip to accept them, and after one or two false starts and whimperings he followed at their heels. They used torches in order to make their way with as little blundering as possible through the grove. Oliphant, who was in the lead, suddenly uttered a violent oath.

"What is it?" Alleyn asked, startled.

"*Gawd!*" Oliphant said. "I thought someone was looking at me. *Gawd, d'you see that!*"

His wavering torchlight flickered on wet willow leaves. A pair of luminous disks stared out at them from the level of a short man's eyes.

"Touches of surrealism," Alleyn muttered, "in Bottom Meadow." He advanced his own torch, and they saw a pair of spectacles caught up in a broken twig.

"We'll pluck this fruit with grateful care," he said and gathered the spectacles into his handkerchief.

The moon now shone on Bottom Meadow, turning the bridge and the inky shadow it cast over the broken-down boatshed and punt into a subject for a wood engraving. A group of tall reeds showed up romantically in its light, and the Chyne took on an air of enchantment.

They climbed the river path up Watt's Hill. Skip began to whine and to wag his tail. In a moment the cause of his excitement came into view, a large tabby cat sitting on the path in the bright moonlight washing her whiskers. Skip dropped on his haunches and made a ridiculous sound in his throat. Thomasina Twitchett, for it was she, threw him an inimical glance, rolled on her back at Alleyn's feet and trilled beguilement. Alleyn liked cats. He stooped down and found that she was in the mood to be carried. He picked her up. She kneaded his chest and advanced her nose towards his.

"My good woman," Alleyn said, "you've been eating fish."

Though he was unaware of it at the time, this was an immensely significant discovery.